OLE

ENGLISH COUNTRY TALES

OLE BISKIT

Jan Stewer

ALAN SUTTON
1987

ALAN SUTTON PUBLISHING
BRUNSWICK ROAD · GLOUCESTER

First published 1925
This paperback edition published 1987
by arrangement with the copyright holders

ISBN 0-86299-432-2

Cover photograph: Jan Stewer in Ole Biskit

Typesetting and origination by
Alan Sutton Publishing Limited
Printed in Great Britain by
The Guernsey Press Company Limited
Guernsey, Channel Islands

CONTENTS

OLE BISKIT

OTHER TALES

CONTENTS

AUTHOR'S APOLOGY

The stories in this book were not written with one eye on the Etymologist. Or perhaps they were, but not in the sense that would be of much use to him; rather in the manner of the schoolboy with a 'Sexton Blake' concealed in his English Grammar keeping an eye on the form-master. They are intended merely for the general (and genial) reader who is willing, and therefore easy, to be entertained and amused. Consequently the text has not been strained, or circumstances created for the purpose of dragging in obscure dialect words of forms. On the contrary I have avoided archaic expressions rarely met with, being content with the language any visitor may hear any day in any Devon village. For the greater comfort of the ordinary reader I have also refrained from extravagant attempts at phonetic spelling which hamper the 'foreigner' without securing correct pronunciation. One realises that all this precludes any value as a work of reference; but as I have neither the skill nor the attainments to produce a work of that sort no dignity so exalted has been contemplated for the present volume. It has, I am bound to confess, no loftier aim than to beguile an idle hour and perchance to gladden the heart of here and there a West-Country exile far from home. If it falls short of that there is no other excuse to offer in its defence.

I mention this to save kindly critics the trouble of pointing out (as hath happened on former occasions) that I have neglected the dialect in this or that particular. I plead guilty to having made the story, such as it is, the first consideration. It has not been written merely to expound the Devon tongue, and if it possess no other interest than that, the book has no justification left.

OLE BISKIT

CHAPTER ONE

Jan fears the 'Evil Eye' of his friends.

I'm being overlooked. That's what I'm being, overlooked.

You can laaf if you like, but I'm jiggered if tid'n getting sayrious. An' what the end aw't will be I don't know; nor I can't think.

You knows what 'tis to be overlooked, daun' 'ee?

'Tis when somebody have got the evil eye upon 'ee, and is ill-wishing of 'ee. And when anybody is ill-wishing of 'ee, all manner of dreadful things hap'ms to 'ee, and you can't avoid 'em, do what you will.

In olden times, if you was being overlooked you went to the White Witch, to vind out who was doing of it to 'ee. Ole Noah Dowslick, what use to live in the little cottage to Orcombe Cross, he was considered to be turrable larnid in all manner of witchcraaf.

Lived in thik zame ole cottage, Noah did, from the day he was born to the day of his death. Dayed in Janawerry, he did, and he'd a-bin one hunderd and vive years old if he'd lived to Michaelmas. That was ole Noah Dowslick, the White Witch.

And the same day as they putt'n to bed with a shool in Orcombe Churchyard, the walls of his cottage tumbled down scat, and the roof valled in. There the ruins be to this day fer anybody to zee. And ev'ry wips-wile, ole Noah hiszel' comes and zits 'pon-tap o' the ruins, raiding out of his ole logic books, and stidding the stars.

There's ever so many volks around thase parts will tell 'ee they've zeed 'n with their awn eyes, although I never glimpsed

1

'n myzel'. But often of a night you can year 'en nooning his ole charms, and 'tis a weesht zound to harken to. Some volks what comes from the towns will tell 'ee 'tis only the weend blawing droo the ruins. But towns-volk will zay anything.

Be-as-twill, people what imagined they was overlooked wude go to ole Noah, and he'd enquire what day o' the wik they was born, and what time o'day 'twas, and then he'd consult his gurt books all about the sky, and the stars, and the planits, and consternations, and comics, and other mysterious things and bim-by he'd come out with the discription o' the body what was ill-wishing aw'm. As a rule 'twould be zomebody thurt-eyed, or 'umpy-backid, or pummle-vootid, and he'd let 'ee have a charm, whereby you could counterac' the evil-eye, and charge 'ee zixpence.

'Tis wonderful what I've knawed poor ole Noah do fer zixpence. Or else he'd charm away yer warts, or let 'ee have a toad's leg to hang around yer neck, and then nobody couldn' overlook 'ee no more. I'll make a bet 'twould surprise anybody to know how many of the ole volks around thase parts has got one of ole Noah's charms around his neck to these day. Although natterally, they'd deny it if you was to ax 'em.

But 'twouldn' be a bit o' gude fer me to go to ole Noah with my troubles, even s'pausing he was alive. Twude only be zixpence drowed away. I daun' need fer nobody to tell me who's over-looking me. I knows it already.

And 'tid'n no enemies, begad. You orwis use to reckon 'twas yer enemies overlooking of 'ee, but with me 'tis me awn friends, and the volks inzide me awn drexil, as the saying is.

And they ban't doing aw't in saycret, nuther. 'Tis all done out in the public eye.

'Jan, you ought to have a moter-car of yer awn,' they said. That's how it started. Fust one said it, and then t'other, till they all said it. 'Jan, why daun' you get yerzel' a moter-car?'

Mrs. Endycott, her started it one day when us was riding back in the ole Carrier's Cart. I'd bin away to zome place down t'other zide o' Plymouth, telling up a few ole ditties as usual to zome kickshaw or 'nother, and 'twas a long ole tayjis journey, sure nuff. I was properly zick, weary and tired o' poking about, changing to one station, and changing to another station, and waiting fer the train zometimes fer howers on end. And that's when Mrs. Endycott said it to me.

2

'Jan,' her said, 'I reckon you should have a moter-car fer yerzel', getting about like you do to zo many different plaaces.'

'Daun' 'ee tell up sitch ole rummidge, missis,' I says. 'Whatever should I do with a moter-car?'

'Do with 'en? Why ride in 'en,' her says. 'You daun' think I meaned fer 'ee to ait 'en, do 'ee?'

'He'd ait me, more likely,' I says. 'You'll be saying next I ought to have a vlying machine, or a subtareen.'

'Well, you never knaws,' her says.

'No, that's very true,' I says. 'Pigs might fly, but they'm most onlikely burds. When you zees me with a moter, then you can expec' the pigs to start sprouting wings any minute.'

Well, and then Mrs. Snell, her cheemed in.

'I dunnaw, Jan,' her says. 'If you was to have a car of yer awn 'twould be a matter o' vine convaynacy to 'ee, wouldn' it, now you'm rinning about so many plaaces, to they ole kickshaws and penny-raidings. Only to zee the different plaaces you have a-bin to laately. All over the shop, ban' 'em?'

'Ees,' I says, 'they'm scattered about a bit. I've bin to Bude, that's right up north o' Cornwall, and down to Penzance, that's so-fur as the train will take 'ee, and scores o' plaaces in between; and up t'other way I bin to Bristol and Bath and Bournemouth and Swindon and lots o' plaaces around there.'

'That's in furrin parts, id'n it?' says Mrs. Endycott.

'Not exac'ly,' I says, 'but getting on that way.'

'What do the missis say 'bout you being away so much?' says Tom Zalter.

'Aw, her says 'tis gude to get a bit o' paice and quietness sometimes.'

'I'll make a bet her do,' says Mrs. Snell. 'I wish you'd take my ole man along with 'ee for a bit, 'genst I've finished the spring-claining. He'm a proper nuisance about the plaace.'

'Well, daun' 'ee find it turrable ockerd getting to some o' the out o' the way plaaces?' says Ned Annaferd.

'I do, zometiimes,' I saith. ''Tis mortle terrifying when you got to bide fer howers to zome li'l ole station waiting fer the train to come along. Darned if I ban't beginning to know all they ole junction plaaces off by 'art where you has to get out from one train and poke about till the nex' one arrives. Like Yeoferd and Halwill Junction, and Yelverton, and Zidmouth Junction, and

3

Lanson, and Par, and ever so many more, and ole Nuton Abbit. Some aw'm be terrible exposed, and if you got to wait fer a nower or zo, the weend cuts 'ee right in two.'

'That's what I say,' says Mrs. Endycott. 'Now if you had a moter of yer awn, you wouldn' want to bother about no trains. You'd simply jump in yer car, go where you wanted to, and jump out.'

'I dersay,' I says. 'But there's a bit too much jumping about it, come to my time o' life.'

'Well, you know what I mean,' her saith.

'I know 'zac'ly what you mean, missis,' I says.

'And 'tis very nice of 'ee and all that, but I reckon it won't be this wik.'

Well, now, you'd 'a-thought that would 'a-bin the end aw't. But bless yer zaul, 'twas only the beginning.

What a vunny thing 'tis, and I expect you've noticed it yerzel'. You hatch up some stoobid ole whim, and fust one body has a go at it, and then another body joins in and adds on a bit more, and then it gets twisted back-an-vore and in-an-out and up-an-down, and it grows an' grows, till to-last, what was started in a joke becomes a sayrious matter. Anyway, I'm blawed if 'twadn' like that with this-yer ole moter-car caper.

When I got home thik night, I mentioned in a jokified soort o' way what Mrs. Endycott shude say, that I mus' have a moter-car.

'Did her say her'd buy 'ee one?' says Ann.

'No, her did'n offer to pay fer't, and I fergot to ax her,' I says.

''Tis worth thinking about,' says the Young Jan.

'Get out with yer nonsainse,' I says. ''Tid'n worth nothing o' the kind. Be you gone mazed too, like the rest aw'm?'

'When you comes to think aw't,' he says, 'you'm spending a middling penny getting about in trains, and you've got to waste a mort o' time sticking about one plaace and t'other. Zee what you'd zave if you could jis flip vore and back in a car.'

'Zave!' I says. 'I shouldn' zave nothing, sep' collers, cus I should break me neck and not want any.'

'Rummidge, break yer neck!' says the Young Jan. 'Why shouldn' you be able to manipilate a car so-well as Roger Laycock? Zee how he gets about in he's.'

'And you could take mother along too, sometimes, fer the ride,' says Jane.

4

'What's that you zay?' says mother. 'Ketch me riding in a moter if yer vather was draiving. He couldn' draive a cat, let alone a car.'

'What do 'ee mean?' I says, 'I dersay I shouldn' be no bigger fule than the rest if I was larned the way proper.'

'I dunnaw who'd larn 'ee, then,' her says. 'I've bin trying to larn 'ee things fer I dunnaw how long, and never succeeded yet.'

Wull, and then us went on yapping, one across t'other, about moters, and this, that and t'other, when who should drap in but Ned Annaferd.

'How be 'ee by this time, Jan?' he says.

'Tired's a dog,' I says. 'I bin trav'ling about all the blessed day till I'm zick aw't.'

'You ought to have a moter,' he saith. ''Twould avoid 'ee a lot o' trouble.'

Then, begad, the vat was in the vire again. Everybody started off to-once.

'Jis' what I've bin telling aw'n,' says the Young Jan. 'My words over again,' says Jane. And mother, her did'n want to be left out aw't so her cheems in with, 'Zac'ly what I was saying as you come in the door.'

Caw! I was properly frightened to year mother say that, cus I did reckon fer certin that her was one on my side. 'Twas like zeeing yer awn ridgement turn tail and join the enemy, as the saying is.

And I never yerd so much conflab about moters in my houze avore. In two minutes they was all discussing what soort o' car I ought to have, and what I should look like sot up in 'en, and what colour he should be, and where us should keep min to, and what clothes mother should wear when her went out in 'en, and what Mrs. Urferd would say when her seed us raiding about in our awn car.

'Fer heab'm's sake,' I says, 'hold thee baal, and not bide there yapping like a passel o' looneys. What's got hold of 'ee, all of 'ee?'

But the harm had bin done. 'Tis a sight aisier to light a vire than what 'tis to make'n out. I was like the man what walked into the river in the dark, and avore he knawed where he was to he was in over head and yers, and the straime carr'ing aw'n away, nobody knows where.

And then, I be dalled, to cap the lot, Jim Cann lookid in zee me on a matter o' business, and almost the fust words he spoke was, 'Have 'ee zeed Squire Potter's new moter-car? My, 'tis a buty, sure 'nuff. He'm wanting to sell his old one I zee. If anybody wanted such thing, now, there's one gwain cheap.'

'Well, look at that!' says Jane. ''Tis like a message.'

And Ann said, ''Tis almost like as if anybody had zeed it in Ole Moore's Ormanick,'

Whatever will be the outcome aw't I dunnaw. Nor I can't think. But what with one and t'other I be in a middling bad way by the looks aw't.

CHAPTER TWO

The agitation for the car increases, and Jan thinks he is being mesmerised.

Things ab'm improved a scrap. What-hever have possessed the volks I can't think, but so-fur as I can zee they've all made up their mind that I be gwain to have a moter-car, if they've got to fetch the king off his throne to do it.

I mind once 'pon a time I was to a party where they got up some ole caper they caaled mesmerising. 'Twas a passel o' tom-fulishness, but some o' the volks believed in it.

What they done was to putt one body outside the rume, and then all the rest concocted what he should do when he come back.

And the way 'twas carr'd out was fer all of 'ee to think hard about what the chap had to do. Keep willing it, you had to, hard as ever you could, and not let yer mind think about nort else. Ned Annaferd was the one to go out the rume, I remember, and 'twas decided that when he come back he should pick up the bellisses off the vloor and hang 'em up to the nail. Nobody muzzen zay a word, but everybody mus' go on thinking till the atmosphere was so full of will-power that Ned would be forced to do what us wanted fer'n to.

Wull, and zo they raycalled 'n in, and us all started to think as hard as ever us cude go. And Ned he stood in the middle o' the vloor, and there was us thinking and thinking, till some o' the volks had got their eyes purt' near jumping out o' their haids with the strain, and to-last ole Ned beginned to move vorrad , and I verily believe he would a-done it, only poor ole Jim Cann, not being accustomed to use his brains to sitch extaint, he thort so hard that he got cramp in his inside. So they had to stap the mesmerising while Jim was being putt to rights, and arter that they was feared to try any more, so it falled through.

7

And upon me zaul, I do believe they'm trying some o' that there mesmerising on me, over this-yer ole moter-car business. It all started with nothing, as you mid say. Only Mrs. Endycott's remark, 'Jan, I reckon you ought to have a moter-car, getting about like you do.'

That's all.

And now, only to zee what it have growed to. Every man, wumman and scraaling cheel in the parrish have tooked it up and joined in the chorriss.

Fust it was, 'Jan, you should have a car.'

Then it was, 'Ullaw, Jan, they tells me you'm gwain to have a car.'

Now, begad, 'tis, 'Gude morning, Mister Stewer. I year you've got a car.'

And the li'l boyes titches their hats to me, if they'm too fur off fer me to raiche.

And tid'n to say 'tis only one yer and there. 'Tis everybody I meets, indoors and out. They'm all alike, the maze-cracks. And my luck's all agin me too. Only one day las' wik, my missis had to go to Kirton Town on a matter o' business. Well, down there where the Young Jan comes from, that's where 'twas. Las' Vridy I think 'twas. Or Zaturday, I dunnaw which. Must a-bin Vridy. No 'twad'n. 'Twas Zaturday, I know 'twas, cus the nex' day was Zindy, and there wad'n no trains to come back by. 'Twas a rare ole roundabout journey, sure nuff, and o' cou'se, they was all telling up the same ole tale.

'There, now. If vather had only got his moter-car he could flip over there with 'ee like winkey.'

Zeeming to me, that's all their idaya, is to zee me go flipping.

Well, and when I had to go out there to Princestown, a day or two agone, there 'twas all over again. A tayjis ole journey that was too. I had to go all out around I dunnaw where to get to it, and all-so-fur back again. Took two whole days to do thik li'l trip. So they all zinged their ole zong again.

'If you only had yer moter-car, zee what difference 'twould a-made.'

'Es, I know,' I says. 'I could 'a-flipped there, couldn' I?'

I be trying my huttermost to vight agin it. But I be like the vox in the hunt, one by mezel', and the whole click agin me. And the wist aw't is, mother's as bad as the rest aw'm. I bleeve her likes to vancy herzel' riding up droo the village and meeting with Mrs. Urferd.

I'm feared of me life to mention that I be gwain anyplace. Somebody sure to say, 'If only you had yer car you could flip there.'

'I dersay he'd be handy,' says mother. 'Zee what us could do if us had one.'

'Ees,' I says. 'Jis zee what you could do. You could drive around the coort to veed the pigs and the poultry, and you could flip up to the pump in 'en, and he'd zave yer legs in gwain back and vore when you was hanging out the washing. I dersay arter a bit you could ride 'n up to bed, and he'd be abble to turn the mangle, and churn the butter, and broom out the back-'ouse arter you'd larned the way to make 'n flip proper.'

But 'tis no gude. I can't radicule 'em to raison. I was a stoobid; I ought to a-bin all in favour aw't, fust start off. Then 'twould a-finished up long ago; cus mother would a-bin opposition as the saying is, and that would a-bin all that was necessary. But I zeldom thinks o' the right thing till 'tis too laate.

And I notice, too, that some aw'm be changing their chune a bit laately. It use to be, *'If* you had a moter-car.' Now, begad, 'tis, *'When* you has yer moter-car.'

And fer certin I shan't have a minute's paice till I goes up to view Squire Potter's ole moter which he'm wanting to dispose of now he've got a new one. That's all the topic now.

Well, I s'pause I can't come to no harm by looking at 'en, if 'twill plaise the volks. But if they thinks I be gwain to do ort so vulish as to purchase a moter-car, they've got the wrong pig by the year. That's all I can tell 'em.

All I 'ope is, that my wive daun' take a vancy to en, that's all. You mid-so-well try to stap to-morrow from coming, as try to stap mother when her've got the maggit biting.

However, I spause we'd better-way go and zee the darn thing, and get it over. And I 'ope he'll bite and kick and bust and gally the life out o' the whole lot aw'm.

CHAPTER THREE

The worst comes to the worst, and Jan finds himself the owner of a motor-car.

I've got a moter-car out in trap-'ouze.

I reckon that won't surprise 'ee very much. You knowed what 'twas coming to for certin.

I was 'feared aw't, mezel'. Hoping and praying fer the best, I was, right up to the very last; but I was 'feared aw't.

When you've got half the parrish up agin 'ee, what can you do? Speshly when the volks in yer awn houze is opposed to 'ee.

However, there the blimming thing stands, out in trap-'ouze, with a grin all over he's vaace every time I goes near 'en, as gude as to say, 'All right, me ole buck, you wait till I gets 'ee out in the midddle of Orcombe Moor. If I daun' pitch you tap-an-tail down over Devil's Burge into the zugs beneath 'tis a wonder to me.'

That's what he'm zaying to hiszel'. I can zee it so-plain as I can zee the viggers on his number. Properly grins, he do, to think what he'm gwain to do to me.

I must tell 'ee how he come to be there I spause.

You know I told 'ee that Squire Potter had bought hiszel' a new car, and offered to zell the old one cheap. Or what he caaled cheap. But I considered 'twas a midddling scute o' money mezel'. However, I promised to look up around and view 'en, and I hoped that would be the end aw't.

And zo it would a-bin, mind you, if only I could have had me awn way. What I wanted to do was to scheme it so's I could go all alone by mezel', and then I could come back and say he was all out o' gear and not worth the money. But it didn ac'. I tried to flip out the door when nobody wad'n looking, but Ann was on me like a burd.

'Where be you gwain with yer best 'at on?' her says.

'I was only jis' gwain to look up around Squire's,' I says.

'Stap a minute,' her says. 'I'll pop on me things and come with 'ee. I wants to zee what soort o' thing us be having avore you lies out all that amount o' money.'

Caw, darn 'ee! I went hot an' cold all ovver. And then the Young Jan cheemed in, 'You'd better-way let me come along too, uncle, cus I knaws a bit about cars, and I could tell 'ee if there was ort radically wrong wai'n. I shouldn' like to zee you get had.'

'Strikes me, young feller-me-lad,' I thinks to mezel', 'that's jis the very thing you *do* want to zee.'

However, I couldn' very well say nay, cus 'twould show that I did'n mean having the car. And then Jane her said her'd like to come along too, and complete the party.

'That's right,' I says. 'And let out the ducks, so's they can volley on behind, and us'll have the Barleycombe town band to go bevore. Mid-so-well do the thing proper.'

'Daun' make yerzel' so stoobid,' says Ann.

'What soort o' feller do you reckon you be to go and choose a moter-car by yerzel'?'

You'll notice it had come to *choosing* a car now.

And so us made up a bit of a precession, and trapesed along to Squire Potter's. And if I'd been the chap they was taking out to Gibbet Moor to be hanged I couldn' 'a-veeled more cheerful than what I did on thikky journey.

All the way out-along they was yapping about what a blessing 'twould be when I had a car of me awn, and what things I could do wai't. 'Pon me zaul, I beginned to wonder how-ever us had managed to knack along so long without one.

And when us got there, Dicky Osegude was waiting to putt the ole car droo his paces, as the saying is. I wish I'd a-thought of seeing Dicky bevorehand. I'll make a bet the car would have had a cold on his chest or zummat, so's he couldn' rin very fur. But I never gets these happy thoughts till 'tis too laate. So there was Dicky doing his uttermost to make out that everything was in apple-pie order, and me trying to ketch his eye to belittle 'en all he could.

Dicky is what they caals 'showfer' to the squire. Drives his car fer 'en, and vrightens the volks out o' zeb'm years' growth around the corners.

11

So he marches us off to the coach-'ouze, or garridge as they caals it, where the moter-car was to.

And only to yer the way they two women-volk did carry on, 'twas nuff to make yer 'air stand up 'pon end. They went 'zac'ly the wrong way to work. Now, if you was buying a hoss, you'd natterally start to rin it down drec'ly, and find all the fau't possible. You'd say he was yaw-neckid, or got ring-bone, or a bit titched in the weend, or a trifle thick about the knees, and a vew more things to knack back the price a bit. And zame by a car. You want to say that the wheels id'n round, or the lid daun' fit on proper, or the hooter id'n loud 'nuff, and vind all the marks you can on the paint and all sitch like. It incourages the chap to knack off a pound or two.

But instaid o' that, they two was praising everything up to the nines. This was mother and Jane, rinning all around the car:

'I reckon he's lovely. A lot better than what I expected. Id'n he you?' 'Yes, ever so much. When he've bin shined up a bit he'll be vit fer anybody to ride in, I'm sure.

'What butiful lamps. They'll glitter like gold with a bit o' brass polish.'

'Come and zee how comferable the sates be. Look how they bumps 'ee up an' down. They must have butiful springs.'

'See what a nice cover to putt up over when 'tis wet. That shows 'tis a gude car.'

'Ees, lookee, and a vine plaace to put yer parcels when you goes shopping. Jis' vancy at that—and a door to go in and out.'

'And a rale mat on the vloor, all vitted to shape. Splendid quality mat too. Do the mat go in with it, young man?' her says to Dicky.

'Aw, yes, missis,' says Dicky, ''tis all exclusive.'

'Then mother her went around and counted the wheels and said they was substantial looking, and that was what her liked about a car. And Jane her blawed the hooter jist as mother was passing in front, and made her jump out of her skeen, purt' near. That gived her zummat else to talk about fer a bit.

But Jane said, 'Can't you zee ole Sophy Grinnaway rishing to look out the winder when her yers us coming along?' And the very thought o' that putt mother to rights again.

And then they went all around and wanted to know what this thing was for, and what that was for, and mother said her'd seed a lot wiss cars than that gwain about, and Jane said her should think her had. With swell people riding in 'em too.

As fer the Young Jan, he was telling to Dicky all about the clitch and the gear and the magneedle and the carbreaker and sparkling plugs and bonnets and caps and jackets and shoes and I dunnaw what-all. Whole suit o' togs, seem-so.

'Have it got all they things?' says Jane. 'Then it mus' be a gude car, fer certin.'

"Tis a turrable lot o' money,' I says.

'Lot o' money?' says Dicky. 'I call he'm giving it away. If squire was to putt a advertyzment on the paper he could make twice the money without turning his hand upzide down.'

'Do 'ee think he would?' says mother.

'I daun' think nothing about it,' says Dicky. 'I tell 'ee one thing, missis. If I had the money to lie out you wouldn't get the chance, cus I should buy 'n mezel', and zell 'en again fer double the profit.'

'I'll lend 'ee the money,' I says, 'if you'll give me a pound out o' what you makes.'

Blowed if that did'n nearly box up Mr. Dicky. He hardly knowed what to zay fer a minute. But of cou'se, you can't get the better of a chap what have had a lot to do with hosses and moter-cars.

'I'd take 'ee on in a minute, Mr. Stewer,' he says, 'only Squire wouldn't like it, cus he said most pa'ticler that you was to have the fust refusal. Matter o' fac', he give me instructions that I was to take 'ee fer a ride if you wished it, so's you could zee how the car do go.'

Caw! That putt the finisher on it. Mother and Jane thought that was a vine idaya. Jane said it showed the squire was honest to let us try it fust, which anybody wouldn' do if there was ort the matter with it. And mother said it wouldn' be like buying a pig in a bag.

So us all got inzide, me in the front sate along o' the driver, and mother and Jane and the Young Jan in behind. I tried to make out there wad'n sufficient rume to be comferable, but they reckoned there was hunderds o' rume, and us could get in one more aisy if everybody was to dispose theirsel's properly.

Dicky twisted round the hannle in front, and all the works inzide started away, rattle-ta-rip, like a drashing machine. Mother

13

thought 'twas winderful that all the different wheels and things should know jis' what to do. Then Dicky jumped up into his sate and pulled a lever or two, and away-da-go, out droo the gate and along the turnpike like a burd flying.

All out droo Week village us went, frightening all the dogs and hens, past Lerberry Cross and Moorget and then around to Orcombe Church Town and down over Orcombe Bottom and up over the steepy bit t'other zide. And mother and the maid behind was spraiding theirzel's out like stag turkeys, to look as prominent as possible, and praying that us might meet with everybody us knawed on the rawd. Mother keeped on to Dicky to blow his ole hooter more often, cus her said her was feared us would rin over zomebody. But 'twas only cus her wanted to attrac' more attention, that's all. And when us did meet anybody her'd go through all the antics imaginable, to avoid being ignored.

As fer me I was trying to make mezel' look so small as I could, and wishing all the time that zummat would break or bust, so's to set 'em agin the darn thing. But nothing never do go wrong when you wants for it to. And us vinished up like a Lord Mayor's Show through Muddlecombe Vore Strate, mother and Jane twisting their haids off, trying to nod both sides to-once.

And when us got home I knawed I might all-so-well go and knock me haid up agin the wall as to say a word agin the ole car. This was mother and the maid:

'Jis vancy! Us have bin tain mile, and it daun' zim no more than crossing the rawd.'

'And comferable! I daun' veel no more tired now than if I'd sot in aisy cheer.'

'Tired! My dear zaul, I veel rested. Us ab'm got sitch comferable cheer in the houze.'

'Don't shake 'ee about like anybody would think, do it?'

'Never shook me a hattom. 'Tis marvellous the way he goes over the bumps.'

'Ees. And the butiful way he turns around the corners. Jis' like anything alive. Shows his guiding part is orright.'

'And what bates me is the way he goes up-heel. He daun' make no more odds to go up-over than what he do down-over, seem-so.'

14

'Anybody daun' seem to mind the noise, do um?'

'I likes it. Makes 'ee think you'm in a train.'

'Anybody would zoon vind it ockerd to be without a car, arter they'd bin use to one fer a bit.'

* * * * *

So now he'm out in trap-'ouze, and all the work o' the place is being niglected while us goes out to gake at 'en vifty times a day.

And tid'n 'trap-'ouze' now, if you plaize. 'Tis 'garridge,' bless yer zaul. I tell 'ee, us be getting on most rapid.

And the nex' thing by all accounts is fer me to larn the way to draive 'en. It putts me all to a sw'at only to think aw't. I tell 'ee I daun' like the way he looks at me.

CHAPTER FOUR

*Contributed by Mrs. Stewer, who does not feel disposed to permit
all her husband's statements to pass unchallenged.*

'Tis a pity my ole man ab'm got zummat better to occupy his
mind than praiching up so much ole rummage about thik blessid
moter-car. If he'd only keep to the truth I wouldn' mind so much,
but most of what he've told 'ee is a paasel o' crams; specially
what he said about me.

Better-fit he was to give his attention to some of the jobs that
wants doing about the place, 'stead o' wasting his time telling so
many fibs.

There's the garden out there, a proper disgrace to the parrish,
which nobody can't deny. And if I've spoke about it once, I have
vifty times. And what do I get fer me pains?

'Aw, I mus' go out and clane up the car a bit.' Or else, 'I got to
make out application fer me lishence,' or, 'I must bump in a vew
stones in front o' the garridge to make it cleaner fer gwain in and
out.'

I've bin platting about in the mud outzide the back-'ouze door
fer years and he've never wanted to bump in no stones fer me to
walk on. But the ole car must have a nice clane path.

Aw, yas. He can idle away half the day tettyvating up his
stoobid car, but if I was to ax 'en to broom out the back kitchen
he'd slatter a bucket o' watter all about the vloor and flick the
broom back and vore a time or two and sprank the vulty watter
all up the walls, and 'twould be vinished in vive minutes. And,
take me till midnight to clane up behine 'en.

But if 'tis his ole car, he'll take every blessed bit o' rag there is
in the plaace, and bissle up every dister I've got if I don't watch'n,
and rub and polish, and puff and blaw and spit fer howers, and
cover hiszel' all over with graise, muck and glory, till he looks like
the Wile Man from Borneo.

16

And he'd drag me out vifty times a day if I was to let'n to, to see what the car do look like when he'm shined up proper. I've got to go zometimes, jis' to humour 'en, else he'd terrify the life out of anybody. And I must zay, he've got'n looking proper vitty.

I said to 'en once, 'If you can shine brass like that,' I said, 'you'd better-way have a go to the warming-pan, and the brass cannle-sticks in the best kitchen, and they milk-pans, and the copper kiddle.'

'I will when I've done this,' he says. 'Not putt yer vingers on 'en, else you'll leave a mark.'

Like a cheel with a new toy, that's what he is, 'zac'ly.

Not that I objec's very much, mind you, 'cus while he'm out there messing about he is out of a body's way. I'd sooner he'd bide out in trap-'ouze shining up his ole rattlebasket as I calls it, than be in yer poking about, hindering anybody in their work, and slammicking back and vore with his muddy boots arter I've washed over the vloor. He id'n doing no hurt out there if he id'n doing very much gude, and I do knaw where to vind 'n if I wants 'en.

Not that us have had much benevit from the moter-car up to now. The blessid thing ab'm turned his wheels around, not 'eet. He ab'm moved outzide the trap-'ouze door since Dicky Ozegude putt'n in. What will hap'm when he do come out gudeness only knows, and I dersay he'm safer where he is. But from what I can make out, vather have got to have a lishence, same's the dog, avore he'm 'lowed to draive the car on the rawd, and he must have'n registered all up to Exeter. What vor I dunnaw. But that's the rules an' reggilations, seem-so.

Middling ole rigmarole to go droo, I'm popped if there id'n, with zo many ole papers all covered all over with questions. Paasel o' stoobid nonsainse I calls it, 'cus it can't be no interest to nobody fer certain. What's the need of it all? There's the car, and if anybody wants to zee what he'm like they can come and look at'n. Nobody ban't gwain to make me believe that there's anybody up to Exeter wants to know what colour our car is, and how many hoss-powers he've got, and how many volks can zit in 'en, and who's gwain to draive 'n, and all sitch matters as that. Vine piece o' chick I calls it, to want to go poking their noses in other volks' business like that. And I shude tell 'em so if 'twas me, County Council or no County Council. Nice thing, arter anybody have paid all that money fer a moter-car, to think that you can't ride in 'en bevore the volks up to Exeter gives 'ee permission.

You never zeed sitch a scummer in all your born days as what 'twas in this houze when vather tried to full in they ole doccy-ments. I thought he would a-went crazy, 'pon me zaul, and everybody else in the plaace along with 'en. He did'n know, no more'n a cat, what answer to putt down to half-quarter o' they questions, and then he'd come out where I was to work and plague me with 'em. Vorty times he carr'd out they ole papers into the kitchen, if he did once, and ax me what I thought he should say. And when I told'n, he wouldn' say it. If he had a-done he'd a-bin locked up I reckon.

'Well, 'tis no use fer you to look to me to help 'ee out aw't,' I says. 'You brought it on yerzel', and you must abide by the consequences.'

I dersay you thinks I be a bit hard on 'en. But you li'l know what I've had to putt up with since thik ole moter-car come puffing and blawing into the coort, drapping oil and graise all over the plaace, and stinking nuff to poison a fitch. I ab'm knowed what 'tis to have a minute's paice from that day to theas. What with he rinning in and out all howers o' the day, taking away all my claining traps jis' when I was gwain use 'em, shabbing off with the scrubbing-brish and me hunting high and low fer 'en, carr'ing away the dishclath, if you plaise, to wipe off they vulty, dirty wheels—well, there!

'Why fer heab'm's sake daun' you ax fer what you wants,' I says, 'not go filching the fus' thing you can lie yer hands upon?'

'I thought 'twas only ole rag,' he says.

'I'll 'ole rag' you,' I says, 'if you daun' leave things bide. You and yer ole car, you'm more plague than profit.'

And then he'd want a bucket fer watter, and then he'd want a clath, and then he'd want a brish, and then he'd come in arter the zoap. And I'm beggered once if I did'n ketch 'en flipping off with my bottle o' furniture crame out o' the drawer o' the back kitchen taable. He was gwain to use that all over the body aw'n, if you plaise, cus he thought 'twould make 'en shine.

'Not fer Jo,' I says. 'If you wants furniture crame at tenpence-ap'my a bottle you buy it yerzel''.'

There id'n a place but what he goes poking his nose to zee what he can furridge out fer his ole car. And now, whenever I

18

wants to use anything I've got to go out in trap-'ouze to vind 'en.

Or 'garridge,' bless yer 'art. That's what us must call 'en now, by all accounts.

Thank gudeness 'twaun' last very long. He'll get a bit more raisonable when the newness have wore off a bit. I've zeed men-volk start on jobs like that bevore.

But what I objec's to most of all is him saying that me and the maid was showing ourzel's off when us was riding around in the car 'long of Urchet Ozegude. If he'd putt it t'other way around there'd be some truth in it. You ought to have zeed the way he was carr'ing on. 'Twas nuff to make a cat laaf. Why, Jane remarked to me herzelf. 'If us meets with many more volks what us knows, vather'll bust.'

Sot up in front he was, along o' the draiver, and me and the maid was sot back behind, so fer certin he couldn' zee what us was doing. But I'm popped if he wad'n dapping up and down like a jack-in-the-box trying to ketch the eye of everybody us passed by.

And who was it axed Dick Ozegude if us couldn' travel out on the Lerberry Rawd, so that us might pass by Jan Grant's place? Did'n tell 'ee that, did he? And what was the business he had to stap and zee Mr. Grant about, when he vound there wad'n nobody looking out to zee us go by? Did'n tell 'ee that, neether, did he? Had'n got no more business with Jan Grant than my voot. Only he must let the ole feller zee that us had come along in a moter-car, that's all 'twas.

And it have been nothing but a precession of volks in and out the place to view the blessid thing. If anybody passes by in the rawd, out he'll go like the spider arter the vly, and fetch 'em in to zee what they thinks aw't. Even had in ole Hoppin' Tom, the drover, he did, and give'n a quart o' zider into the bargin, cus the ole feller said that the man what purchased thik car wad'n no fule. And I daun' suppose Hoppin' Tom knows the vore end of a car from the back end. But 'e knows who keeps gude zider, and he's as gude a jidge of a fule as most people.

But as I zay, if you wanted a bit o' fun you ought to a-zeed the rigs us had over they registration doccyments. I suppose Jan thought, being innocent like, that all you had to do was to pay yer money fer the car and then get up and ride about in 'en. But the policeman soon putt'n to rights about that.

'Squire ab'm had thik car registered,' he said, 'cus he ab'm use 'n since the new reggilations come in power. You'll have to get'n registered.'

'That's orright,' says Jan, 'nobody id'n gwain to bother their haids about reggilations out yer to Muddlecombe. 'Tid'n as though I was gwain to make 'n go vast. 'Twill be surprise to me if I make 'n go at all.'

'Aw, that id'n no gude,' says the policeman. 'You'll have to have yer lishence. A moter-car id'n like a gun, yer know. You can't flip around behind a hay-rick if you zees anybody coming.'

'You dunnaw what I shall be abble to do when I starts to drive,' says Jan. 'I dersay I shall flip around behind a gude many things, whether there's anybody coming or no.'

However, vather had to send up to Exeter fer the proper papers; and 'twas titch-and-go whether he wouldn' have to be putt away to lunatic 'zylum long bevore he answered all they questions which had to be fulled in.

I can't mind 'em all now, 'cus 'twas mostly double Dutch to me. But I knaw one thing, us had to putt down what colour his body was. I mean the car's body, not Jan's. Us had a long ole argimentation about that, and to-last us all went out to have a good look at'n and dezide.

I reckoned he was yaller, but they wouldn' agree to than, and I must say, when you come to putt zummat yaller up agin 'en he did'n zeem to match it very well.

'Well, say a soort of dirty yaller,' I says.

'I shan't say nothing o' the kind,' says Jan. 'He must be a colour o' zome soort.'

'Call 'en stone colour,' says the Young Jan.

'What's the gude o' that?' says Jan. 'I've zeed stones that is red and I've zeed stones that is blue.'

'If you was to say, "bathbrick,"' I says, "twould jist about do it.'

'Tid'n a matter fer radicule,' says Jan. 'If you can't talk sainse bide quiet.'

Getting proper wopsy he was.

'What about "buff"?' says Jane.

'Enough about it,' says vather. 'There's no sitch colour as bluff.'

'Her did'n say "bluff,"' I says. '"Buff," her said.'

'And "Stuff" I says,' says Jan. '"Stuff and nonsense." With yer "buff"! Mid-so-well call 'n "muff," or "duff."'

20

Well, so then us called in Sophy Grinnaway, her being a dressmaker, and expert as regards to colours.

'Why, 'tis biskit colour,' says Sophy, drec'ly.

'Of cou'se 'tis biskit,' says Jane. 'Vancy us not thinking o' that.'

'Well, he takes the biskit anyway,' says the Young Jan, 'so he ought to be that colour.'

So, 'Biskit' was wrote down on the paper, and the ole toad was called BISKIT from that day forth, and he've gone by that name ever since.

But the most upstore of all was over the size of his ingine, which had to be wrote down likewise. From what I can make out you has to pay tax according to the size of the ingine.

Of all the capers that was the masterpiece, and I thought Jan would have drove us all mazed.

'How do I know the size of his blimming ingine?' he says.

'Well, measure 'en to be sure,' I says.

'All very well to say "measure 'en,"' he says. 'Where be I gwain to measure 'en to?'

'Why, from one end to the t'other, o' cou'se,' I says.

'I ban't so sure I knows which is the ingine,' he says.

'You'm a bright buty to have a moter-car,' I says. 'Supposing I was to say I did'n know which part of the mangle was the rollers.'

Well, so then Jan had in the blacksmith and axed he what measurements he reckoned the ingine was. And he said he considered 'twas up two voot, or thereabouts. So Jan said he reckoned there mustn' be no "thereabouts."'

'Why daun' 'ee go up to squire's and enquire of Dicky Ozegude?" I says.

Aw, he had'n thought o' that. So off he goes to the Manor, but Dicky couldn' tell'n nothing, cus you had to measure his inzide, seem-so, and to do that you mus' take 'n all abroad.

'The only way is fer you to write a letter to the makers,' Dicky said.

So Jan had to do that, and a purty vine ole scummer 'twas, too, fer the Young Jan wad'n yer to help 'n, and he wouldn' putt down what I said. However, I suppose the makers must a-guessed what he required, cus they send back some viggers which us couldn' make tap ner tail o', and Jan copied 'em down on his ole paper. I know 'twas dree inches and a bit, and 'twas supposed to be the size of a boar. More like a mouse, I said, than a boar.

21

Be-as-twill, I was very glad to zee the last o' thik paper, I can tell 'ee, when father putt 'n in the post.

And when it come back, what do 'ee think there was to pay? That's only fer tax, mind.

Twainty-one pound!

Twainty-one pound, 'pon tap of what us had paid already.

My gudeness gracious!

Twainty-one hosses power they said 'twas, and you have to pay a pound a hoss, sim-so. But I'll never believe it. Anyway, I know which I'd soonest have, and if I couldn' do more with twainty-one hosses than he can do with thik car I'd ait 'em, tails and all. And what I can't make out about they Exeter lot, you sends up fer one boar, and a li'l teeny-weeny one at that, and they charges 'ee fer twainty-one hosses. 'Tis all wrong.

You mid depaind vather did'n get very much paice that morning.

But what do 'ee think he said?

'Aw, well,' he says, 'if 'tis all that money fer dree inches and a bit, let's be thankful us did'n send up the blacksmith's two voot or thereabouts.'

However, that's all I've got to zay. And I shouldn' a-thought that having a car about the plaace could have upzet anybody's home like it.

CHAPTER FIVE

Jan learns that driving a car is not as easy as it looks.

You knowed already that I was a bit of a stoobid, from what I've told 'ee in the past. And what I've left out mother have putt in.

And I knowed it mezel', too, which is more than a gude many can zay. But if I had'n knowed it bevore, there's a plenty has been only too aiger to invorm me laately.

Not that it would have been necessary at all, 'cus I very soon discovered what a fule I was when I tried to larn the way to drive thik ole moter-car.

In the very fus' place I was a fule ever to purchase the blimming ole thing at all, or to have ort to do wai't. They say that knowledge bought is better than knowledge taught, so mine ought to be purty gude, begad. I bought it orright, and paid big money for't.

Whether 'tis any value to me now I've got it is another matter.

Anyway, it have larned me one thing which I s'pose I ought to 'a-knowed bevore. And that is not to jidge by appearance.

How many times have I zeed volks gwain off fer a ride in their moter-cars, and I've thought to mezel' how aisy 'twas. Nothing to do, I use to think. They'd jis' give a bit of a twist around to the hannle in front, and then dap up in their sate, and away-da-go, aisy as winky. Many's-a-times I've passed the remark that 'twas a sight more convaynient than harnessing a hoss and trap. Not half the bother, and twice as quick.

And then, only to zee 'em getting about. They'd rin along so suant, without so much as spaiking to, and flip in and out between the travvic, and go vore or back, or turn around the corners, jist as they mind to.

That's what I use to think. But I'm wiser now. I've larned that you muzzen jidge cars by their looks any more than passens by their books. I use to think you only had to turn a wheel or push a button and the blessed thing would do whatever you mind fer'n to. But you won't yer me talk like that in future. I dersay I'm jist as fulish now as I was tho, but 'tis in a different way. There's the fule that daun't knaw, and the fule that do knaw. I'm the fule that do.

I've had jibbing hosses bevore now, and other contr'y baists, like pigs and calves. And I once had to do with mules fer a bit, which has fergot more wickedness than the rest o' the baists ever larned. But I never come across no animal that could be so stubborn and contr'ywise as what a moter-car can. Not even a wumman, and that's saying summat.

A wumman will give 'ee some soort of a raison fer what her will do and what her waun' do, even if there id'n much sainse in the raison. But a car's different. If he waunt he waunt, and there's end to it.

And you can argify with a wumman, even if there id'n nothing to be got by it. But 'tis a bit o' satisfaction, and her's orwis raddy to argify back again.

But you can't argify with a car, and you can't raison with 'en, and you can't shame 'n. And if you kicks 'en, you'm more likely to hurt yer own veelings than he's. And I tell 'ee straight I've bin tempted to do that more'n once.

And I've knowned hosses bevore now what could tell in a minute who was driving aw'm. One body could hannle 'em as aisy as turning yer hand up-and-down, and make 'em do jis' what he mind to. And with others they'd be as contr'y and pig-haided as ever possible.

Ole Biskit's like that, zac'ly. When the Young Jan's driving aw'n he can't do nothing wrong. You'd think he was all the time on his way to Zindy-skule. He'll go along as gude as gold, and never look to the right hand ner to the left.

But the minute I takes 'n in hand to try to make 'en do ort, he turns zulky, and do's zac'ly the oppozyte. Or else he waun' do nort, but jis' stands there laafing to me. If I tries to make'n go vore he'll rin back and push over the gaate-post. And if I wants 'n to come'eer he'll wug-auf, and poke his nawse in the haidge-traw as though he was chasing a rabbut.

I shall never be abble to drive thikky car proper, I know I shan't, not so-long as I've got a nawse in me faace.

The Young Jan have properly got the knick of it. He know'th 'zac'ly which hannle you must pull to and which you must push

24

to, and what thing you must squeeze with yer veet. And he can
make Ole Biskit twist about jis' where he minds fer'n to, or go droo
the eye of a needle. I bleeve he could make'n zit up and beg, or rin
around arter his tail if he mind to. But he waun' do nothing fer me,
seps what I daun' wish fer'n to.

Cou'se, the boye tries to comfert me.

'Twill come in time, uncle,' he says. 'You'll break 'n in, arter a bit
more practice.'

'He'll break me in fust,' I says. 'Break my neck, that's what he'll
do.'

You zee, where 'tis to, 'tis like this-yer. When you'm driving the
ole car there's a sight more things to think about than anybody
would imagine. As I zay, when I use to zee the volks flipping about I
use to think that all you have to do was to let'n go and keep'n
straight. And I reckoned any fule could do that.

But laur bless yer zaul, tid'n so. You'm all the time on the go with
zummat. There's wheels yer, and hannles there, and levers
someplace else, and there's jobs fer yer veet to do, and my poor ole
head waunt hold it all. Not and mind where I be gwain to at the
same time.

The Young Jan says 'twill all come natteral arter a time, but I'm
feared 'twill be a mortle long time.

Fust you got to wind 'n up in front, to make the ingine go, and
that id'n half so aisy as what it do look. I use to think it wad'n no
more strength than giving a couple o' turns to the turmit-cutter. But
'tis a sight more like the last pull on the zider-press. Cou'se 'tis only
a matter o' getting the knick aw't. The Young Jan can do it as aisy
as mother turns the churn. He'll give'n a jit or two, and away goes
the ole ingine, rattle-ta-rip, like's if he was shaking hiszel' to bits.

But I ab'm got in the way aw't. 'Tis much as ever I can do to
move the ole hannle around, and he waunt rattle fer me. He might
p'r'aps give a cough or two, and spit a bit, but nothing more.

Not that yer troubles is ended even when you do make the ingine
start. Matter o' fac', that's when they begins. You got to nip up in
yer sate and do several things, and fer the life o' me I can't keep in
me haid what 'tis I got to do. There's too much to think about.

Fust of all there's a thing caaled acsillyrater which you mani-
pilates with yer voot. Well, I can do the ac' silly part all right. That's
all I zim to do, ac' silly. I squeezes 'en down when I ought to have 'n
up, and I lets 'n up when he ought to be down. 'Tis all very well to

25

say you've only got to do this, that and t'other, but when you'm
fiddling about different things with yer hands 'tis a job to mind what
yer veet be doing at the same time. This yer acsillyrater turns on the
gas, sim-so, and I sure to make 'n go quick when I ought to make 'n
go slow, and then if there's aught in the way there's boun' to be a
bust-up.

Well, and then there's a thing caaled a clitch, which you mus'
keep squeezing down with the t'other voot. And in between they
two is the gadjit what works the brake. So anybody railly wants dree
veet to do the thing properly. What the clitch is vor I dunnaw. But I
do knaw that if you daun' trait'n proper he'll very soon get 'ee in
trouble.

Fer the life o' me I couldn' remember to putt me voot on the
clitch at the proper time, and then all of a sudden you'd yer sitch a
noise in Ole Biskit's inzide you'd think he was coming all abroad.
Make anybody veel as if he was gwain up and never coming down
again. The Young Jan said 'twas his teeth, but I'd never think
anything could do that with his teeth. Sounded to me more like's if
his bowels was being tore out.

And you was jist as bad off if you push 'n down the wrong time. I
knaw, cus the ole clitch got on my mind to sitch extaint that I putt
me voot on 'en wai'out thinking, and the Ole Biskit wouldn' go at
all. He won't if you pushes the clitch down. Well, and not thinking
what I was doing I putt me other voot on the acsillyrater, and away
goes the ole ingine, roaring like thinder, but the car not moving.

Cou'se, away goes my wits, out droo me hat, and not knowing
what to do else I pushes both veet down hard. Natterally I was
letting in full quantity o' gas, and having no work to do, being that
I'd got the clitch down, away goes the ingine, rattle-ta-rip, nuff to
shake all the teeth out of yer haid. And bevore the Young Jan could
tell me what to do nex', I lifted up both me veet, and Ole Biskit give
one jump and then stapped daid, ingine and all. Anybody could tell
'twas a turrable shock to his system.

'Now, what have I done?' I says.

'I've told 'ee ever so many times,' says the boye, 'that you
muzzen let her start when you'm in tap gear. You mus' putt her in
bottom gear fust.'

That there ole gear business alone is nuff to drive anybody
mazed, never mind all the other fakements. I shall never larn the
way aw't if I live to be as old as Methusalum.

You zee, when you'm driving a hoss he'll natterally start away aisy of his awn accord, and then if you wants to go a bit vaster you jis' spaiks a word to 'en, or give'n a snick with the whip and he'll trat or gallup or whatever you mind for 'en to. And when 'tis collar work he'll slow up and go stiddy without you bothering yer haid.

But tid'n like with a car. You got a thing caaled a gear, with a long hannle down by yer zide, which you must keep manoovering about, according whether you'm gwain vast or slow. And if you daun' manoover 'en right you'll tear his inzide all abroad. There's bottom gear and sacond gear and tap gear. Likewise there's reverse gear and nootral, which is no gear at all. And one hannle do's the lot, according which crevice you putts 'en into. And if you don't call that's too much fer one man to keep in his haid, bezides minding the clitch and the acsillyrater and the brakes at the zame time and also thinking about where he'm gwain to and what he'm rinning into, then you'm a lot wiser than what I be, that's all.

So fur as I'm consarned, I eetherways don't make 'n go at all, or I makes 'n jump out of his skeen, or else I fergets to guide'n straight and he rins into the haidge-traw, 'side the rawd.

And o' cou'se, mother her's watching it all from the coort and her goes fer me like a pickpocket.

'I can't think for the life o' me what makes you so stoobid arter you'm told what to do. There's all the things there to do it with, what more do 'ee want? You've got hannles in galore, and the boye keeps telling 'ee what to do with 'em. I can't understand why you'm so ockerd.'

'Well, you come up yer and shaw us how 'tis done,' I says. 'You'm so vast about vinding fau't, let's zee what you can do towards it.'

'I'll make a bit I'd take a better hand to it than what you do,' says mother. 'And 'tis no gude you getting wopsy. You can't help being sitch a gawk I daun' suppose.'

'Mother, you shouldn' say such things when vather's doing his best,' says Jane.

'Well, if that's his best,' her says, 'caal me out again when he'm doing his worst, and I'll come and gather up the oddments.'

But I'd had nuff fer once. They putt away the ole car and shut up the door, and I never zeed the toad again for dree days. Cude'n a-bear the zight aw'n.

CHAPTER SIX

Jan gets instruction in the art of driving, with simple explanation of the use of the speed gears, clutch, accelerator and so on. He says 'Yes,' but is not very clear on the matter. He goes out for his first driving lesson.

Anybody need to be very careful how they laafs at the fulish, cus they might get struck like it theirsel's one day. There's more than one has laafed at me trying to drive thik car, but if they'd bin through what I went through they'd bin more fit to cry than laaf.

As I told 'ee bevore, I got 'artily zick an' tired o' the zight o' the ole moter-car, fus' time I tried me hand with'n. Mind you, that wad'n a proper trial, cus I'd only got the width o' the road to travel in, and not a very wide road at that. But 'twas wide nuff to let me zee that Ole Biskit wouldn' do nothing that I wanted for 'en to. He'd made up his mind to that. And no matter where I tried to make 'n go, he'd go zacly oppozyte.

So I said, 'Us'll stick the ole contraption back in trap-'ouze (or garridge as us must caal'n now) and let'n set a bit till he comes to his sainses.'

So us putt'n in garridge, and I never so-much as zeed 'n fer days. The Young Jan took'n out a time or two, I believe, and by all accounts he could make'n do any mortle thing. But I tell 'ee, Ole Biskit had took a dislike to me. I knaw he had. I could veel it in me boans.

However, one day the boye said to me, 'You've got to larn the way to drive 'n sooner or later, cus you can't go and pay all that money fer'n and then not use'n. You'd be the laafing stock o' the parrish. You'd master 'en quick enough, if you putt yer mind to it, same's any other body. Us'll take'n right out on the moor,' he says, 'where us can't hurt nobody, and in one-hower you'll be draiving so-well as the next.'

Wull, it did'n zeem hardly worth-a-while to waste all that money fer nort, so I said I'd have one more go at'n.

28

But look yer,' I says, 'if he waun' do what I wants fer'n to thees time, I'll get rids o' the toad. I'll zell'n again. And if I can't zell'n, I'll give'n away to zomebody I owes a gridge to.'

Wull, zo the boye went out to get the car all in raddiness, and give'n a drink o' petrol, and putt some oil in his innerds, and puff a bit o' weend in the wheels.

'Now, lemme zee,' he says, 'is there anything else?'

'Ees,' I says. 'Putt a kicking-strap on the old baiste.'

Wull, then, Young Jan he lifts up the lid and starts to viddle about with zummat in under.

'What be on upon now?' I axed 'n.

'Flidding the carbraker,' he saith.

'What's that for?'

'To make'n start aisy.'

'Then let'n bide, thee gurt mump,' I says. 'Us daun' want nothing to 'sist 'n to start. 'Tis summat to make 'n stap us wants.'

'Aw, that's orright,' he saith. 'You can use a hayrick fer that, same's you did bevore.'

'I'll give you a bump in the back if you ban't careful, young feller-me-lad,' I says.

However. He give a bit of a twest around to the hannle in front, and Biskit he spit a time or two, and then, all of a zudden, away he goes, rattle-ta-rip, as if he was gwain to rish right around the world. But not moving an inch. Only his inzide rattling as if he'd bin aiting zummat that disagreed wai'n.

You zee, 'tis orwis like that. When you ordains riding in a car, you starts his works off independent, like. He'm only rinning by his mind, as the saying is. Like when the ole dog's asleep and draiming he's arter a rabbut, he puffs and blaws, and grints and potes, but he daun' get no forrader.

Well, then, when you've got his inzide rattling in a proper manner, you mus' dap up into yer seat and frig about wi' the hannles an' the levers, and push down the clitch, and half-dizzen more things, and if you do's 'em all proper, he'll start off nice and suant, and away-do-go like winky.

But if you daun' do it right, look out. He'll jump and kick and grind his teeth and back up agin the wall; or else he'll stap daid, sulky as a pig. And then you got to get out and twest around his inzide all over again.

However, 'twas the boye draiving, not me. Zo I zot down beside 'n.

'Now,' he says, 'you watch and zee what I do, and then you can do likewise, bim-by. Now, then, what be us in now?'

'In trap-'ouze,' I says.

'No, no—'

'Well, garridge, then. 'Tis all the zame, stoobid.'

'I daun' mean that. What gear be us in?'

'Aw, gear! I did'n understand what you meant. What gear be us in? Well, jidging by the racket, I should say us be in several.'

'No, giddout,' he says. 'Us can't be in more than one to-once. Which is it? High, low, sacond, or what?'

Well, I thought I'd better-way say zummat, so I said 'High,' I reckoned he'd do so-well as any.

'No, no, no!' he says. 'Ab'm I told 'ee scores o' times that if us was in high us would be licking along like one-a-clock?'

'Low,' I says. I thought he mus' be one or t'other.

'No, uncle. If 'twas low, us would be gwain along very slaw pace, or up a steep nap.'

'Well, us'll say, 'bout of a happy mayjim then,' I says, jis to plaize the feller.

'Aw, come now, uncle,' he says. 'I explained it all to 'ee t'other day. When the car's stood still and his inzide is working—'

'Aw, I knaw!' I says. 'Stap a minute. I've got it on the tip o' me tongue. 'Tis neuralgia, or nuisance or somethin' like that. Numatic?'

'Neutral,' he saith.

'Ay, that's of it. I knowed 'twas summat new. That's right, neutral. Wull, go on.'

'Wull now,' he saith. 'Bevore you starts you'm into neutral. Then you shoves down the clitch with yer voot, like that-there, zee, and putt this-yer lever into low gear, like so. That's aisy nuff, id'n it?'

'Any fule could do that,' I says.

'Wull, he'm in gear now, look-zee, all ready to start, and if I was to take up me voot off the clitch he'd begin to move slow. Then I shall shove down the clitch again and change the lever from low gear to secon' gear, and he'll go vaster. Then I shall do zame again and change to tap gear, and he'll lick along nice and suant. Nort very difficult about that, is 'er?'

'Aisy as looking droo a ladder,' I says.

So then he done what he said he would, and me watching all the manoovers, same's I'd done a dizzen times bevore. And as I zay, 'twas

30

all so zimple as drinking a jug o' zider. Jis' push with the lef' voot, shove the ole hannle in his plaace, then let up the lef' voot and dap down the right one, and there you be. You'd think a cheel vive years old couldn' make a mistake, to zee another body do it. Us travelled out in coort, and droo the vore-gate, and turned in the rawd, zac'ly zame as if Ole Biskit had knawed where he was gwain to. And then us went licking along, jis like one train.

'All you've got to think about now, uncle, is the guiding wheel and this-yer li'l pedal under yer right voot. You minds what he'm called, daun' 'ee?'

'Ees,' I said.

'What's he called?'

'Wull, I *did* knaw, but I've fergot fer the minute. You can't expec' me to mind everything fus' gwain off.'

'That's the acsillyrater,' he says.

'That's right,' I says. 'I had it on the tip o' me tongue.'

'And what's he for?' says the boye.

'To make 'ee go at a silly rate.'

'He controls the amount o' gas you'm putting in the ingine,' he says.

'That's what I was jis' gwain to zay.'

'Now, you zee,' says the boye, 'when I presses he down us goes vast, and when I lets 'n up us goes slaw.'

And so us did, begad. 'Twas aisy as kiss yer 'and. Jis' dap yer voot on the acsillyrater, and away-do-go like winky. Take 'n up, and you wouldn' ketch vore to a funeral.

But I knowed very well in me awn mind he wouldn' do like that fer me. If I wanted for'n to go slaw he'd go rishing about like a hen with a strange doug. And if I tried to make'n go vast he'd stop daid.

Yet there us was, flipping along so suant, and keeping nice in the middle o' the rawd, and Ole Biskit did'n want to look in over the gates, ner putt one wheel in the haidge-traw, ner nort. And the Young Jan never need spaik a word to 'en. Jis' turning his guiding wheel a bit, and sot back smocking his pipe, and telling away, as if us was sot in chimley corner. And Ole Biskit coosing along like a burd vlying.

And I knawed, as well as I knawed me awn name, that the minute I tried to do it, the ole toad would get as contr'y as a calve in the middle of Exeter High Strate. He'd want to zee how the

31

crops was getting on in every vield he come to. He'd want to stop and rade all the derecting paustis, or ait grass by the zide o' the rawd. He'd try to go thurtways or backseyvore, andd if he could throw me out, haid voremost, into the zugs, nothin' wouldn' plaise'n better.

And when us got out on the moor the boye said, 'Now, uncle, come and zee what you can do towards it.'

'Never mine, now,' I says. 'You'm getting on very well. Bide on as you be.'

'Giddout,' he says. 'Us have come yer for you to larn the way to draive. Now's the time.'

And with the zame he brought Ole Biskit to a stan'still, and made rume fer me to sit in draiver's plaace. 'Twas no use fer me to make excuses or try to get out aw't. He was determined that I shude draive thik car or bust in the attemp', as the saying is. And so I moved up into the draiver's sate.

I've yeard that in America the mudderers sits in a cheer to be executed, and I knaws exac'ly how they veels, cus I veeled like it that minute. I had the sinsation that if I moved hand or voot, the whole blessid lot wude go up in the air, like when they'm blasting gurt rocks to the quarry.

Ole Biskit's ingine was wizzing around in his inzide, only waiting fer the opportunity to dash haidlong to perdition. I was 'fraid to titch a thing, feared I'd give'n excuse to be off.

I dersay you'm laafing up yer sleeve, and thinking what a stoobid ole toad I be. But I tell 'ee straight, 'tis a weesht soort o' veeling when you'm gwain to start off a ramping, roaring wile-baist on vower wheels, what can flip along like graise' lightning, and you dunnaw when you'm gwain to stop again, or whether you'll ever stop again or no.

You zee, a moter-car id'n same's a hoss. A hoss have got two eyes in his haid, and some sainse of his awn. He can zee fer hiszel' if there's aught in the way, and he've got the gum'tion to stap, or turn to one side. But this-yer crack-brain ole contraption, I knowed very well he had'n got the sainse of a louse. He was only waiting fer the chance to go like a bull at a gate. Whatever might be in the rawd he wouldn' turn left ner right. 'Twould be jist his han'writing to go slap-bang into the fus' thing he come to. I knowed it would.

However, there 'twas. The Young Jan had lef' 'en nice an' straight in the middle o' the rawd, an' 'twas fer me to make'n go vore.

'Now, uncle, 'tis as aisy as valling off a rick. All you got to do is to shove down the clitch with yer voot, putt the lever in low gear, then take up yer voot gradule and putt t'other one on the acsillyrater. And then he'll start by hiszel.'

And zo he did. I be jiggered if he did'n.

I shoved me voot down hard 'pon the knob, and putt the lever where he said I was to.

'Now let up yer voot,' he says, 'and push down the acsillyrater a bit, and watch where you'm guiding to.'

Well, I spause, being a bit over-anxious, I did'n let up the clitch 'ardly gentle enough. Matter o' fac', I tooked me voot off right away, and let'n come up scat. And with the zame I pushed the acsillyrater down hard, which o' cou'se turned on all the gas us had got.

Man alive! Ole Biskit give one jump, and away-do-go like a race-oss. I went pins and needles all over. Tell about watching where I was guiding to. I wad'n guiding nowhere. I olleyed out 'Woa! Git back!' But the blimming ole toad was kicking up sitch a clatter he couldn' year what I said, and he rattled on like one train.

Guide 'n straight, uncle,' says the boye. 'You'm doing all right. Turn the wheel a bit.'

I turned the wheel all right. In me excitement I turned 'n a bit too hard. Ole Biskit flipped his haid around, only too glad o' the excuse. He kicked up his hine wheels, and he shot off the side o' the rawd right out on the moor. My dear life! I started pushing and pulling everything I cude reach to vind zummat to stop 'n with. But I only made it worse.

Barleycombe steeplechases wad'n in it. Us was bumping over humps and stoans, and jumping ditches, and I was jis' 'pon the point of dapping out over the zide to zave me life when the Young Jan titched zummat that fetched the rinaway to a stan'still with his nawse in a gurt vuz-bush.

'That's nuff fer me,' I says. 'I waun' draive'n no more. You can do what you mind to. I tell 'ee I waun' draive 'n no more. He'm properly wicked, I knaw he is.'

'Giddout, wicked,' says the boye. 'That was all right.'

'All right!' I says. 'Wull, if that was all right 'twill be worth zeeing when 'tis all wrong.'

'Tid'n gwain to be all wrong,' he says. 'You let the clitch up a bit too coose, that's all. You'll do vine nex' time.'

So then he got the car back on the rawd again.

33

'Now,' he says, 'take yer voot up a bit more aisy this time, and let'n start gradule.'

Wull, zo I did. I let up me voot as gentle as possible, and nothing did'n hap'm fer a bit. So I was in hopes that zummat had gone wrong with the works, and I shouldn' be abble to draive'n 't all. I let'n up a trifle more and the begger beginned to movee. So I dap'n down again quick, and he stopped with the zame.

'That's right, uncle, you was doing butiful. Let'n come up again, and keep'n straight with the guiding wheel. Jis' give a titch to the acsillyrater, and that'll keep 'n gwain.'

Zo I did, and bim-by us beginned to movee nice and suant.

'That's lovely, uncle. Keep'n to that and guide'n straight.'

But you tell about guiding straight! Might jis'-so-well try to drive the ole zow straight where her daun' wish to go, as thik blessid car. Darn if he did'n want to zee everything that was gwain on, both zides o' the rawd. Fust he'd go over one zide to zee how many miles 'twas to Plymouth. Then he'd flip across t'other zide to rade the derecting paust. Then he'd want to go picking primroses, or poke his nawse in a rabbut-'ole. Any mortle thing he'd do, 'sep go where I wanted for'n to. And there was me, twisting the ole wheel vore and back, sw'atting strames, and expecting every minute he'd take it into his haid to lay down and roll over on his back.

My dear days! 'Twas a hawful sinsation. I veeled like's if I had'n got a particle o' control over nothing. Us was slipping and sliding and womm'ling about, and I was panking and blawing, with me 'art in me mouthe and me eyes like tay-sassers. I knaw they was. I wanted to stap the ole nuisance, but I did'n knaw which way to, and I was feared o' me life to titch any o' the hannles and things, feared I should cause 'n to do zummat rash. I couldn' zee nothing else for it but to go on till us meet with zummat big 'nuff to stap us.

And then, wai'out thinking what I was doing I shoved me voot down on the clitch, and us come to stan'still.

And when I lookid around to the Young Jan, what's think he was up to? He was sot back in his seat laafing like one o'clock. Laafing fit to bust hiszel' he was. Made me a bit narked, I can tell 'ee.

'Zummat to-laaf about, id'n it?' I says, a bit sharp like.

''Twas fus' rate, uncle,' he says. 'You'm getting on vine. But 'twould make a cat laf to yer you telling to Ole Biskit.'

'What do 'ee mean, telling to 'en?'

34

'Why, all the time coming along you've bin holleying out, "Com'eer, Biskit, you ole toad, you. Wug back. Biskit, my dear! Stiddy, you ole stoobid. Wug-aaf! Woa! Com'eer! Biskit-ah!"'

And then he lied back and roared laafing. But I very soon putt a stop to that. Of cou'se, all this time I'd had me voot on the clitch, and without thinking what I was doing I took 'n off. My hivers! Away goes Biskit, like a shat out from a gun, straight as a line fer a stoanen gate-paust, stood up by the zide o' the rawd. In one minute us would a-bin scat all to flibbits, cus I did'n knaw what to do, no more'n a cat. But Young Jan he jumped to the wheel, and guided n' around jist in the nick o' time. 'Twas a near nip, 'pon me zaul.

'Simmin' to me,' I says, 'this-yer car be simply watching fer chance to commit suicide.'

'You muzzen never let'n bide in gear, like that, uncle,' he says. 'When you stops you mus' putt'n into neutral, and then he can't start avore you putts'n in gear again.'

'There's too many things to mind in this caper,' I says. 'My haid will never hold 'em all, ner 'eet half of 'em.'

'Rummage,' he says. 'Arter a time or two you'll do 'em all as natteral as finding yer mouthe in the dark. Now start'n again. You'm doing splendid.'

'I'd like to knaw what you calls splendid,' I says.

However, I had a go at'n again, and this time I knawed a bit what to expec', so twad'n so bad. The Ole Biskit moved off so-suant as a train.

'That's proper uncle. Now putt'n in secon' gear. Shove down the clitch, let up the acsillyrater, shift the lever, then let up the clitch again and open acsillyrater.'

Sounds all right, and you'd think any fule cude do it. And I could do it mezel' when us was stood still. But when you got to guide the ole consarn into the bargain, and you knaws that if you titches the wrong thing you'm gwain to Halifax, it makes 'ee go preckles all over. However, I did zummat which I thought was right thing, and I gived a pull to the hannle, much harder than what I intainded.

Caw! Dear 'art alive! I thought 'twas earthquake. Biskit stapped daid, like's if he'd run slap into a stoanen wall. Purt' near sent the pair of us clane droo the glass winder. And then, I'm beggered if the ole toad did'n fling hiszel' right around, hind part bevore, so's us was looking back the way us come. Ingine and all stopped,

35

and fer a minute 'twas quiet as death. Neether-one aw's had'n got breath to spaik.

'What fer heab'm's sake have I done now?' I says to-last.

Then the Young Jan beginned to laaf again.

'Done!' he says. 'Why, you pulled the wrong hannle and put on the brake.'

'But what have he turned around fer? Is it feeding time with 'en, and he wants to go home?'

''Twas stopping so sudden,' he says, 'and the graise on the rawd made'n slip around. Gude job us wad'n gwain vast.'

'Better-fit us wad'n gwain 't all,' I says. 'Seeming to me, no sooner I overcomes one thing than he invents zummat fresh. You come and draive the baistly thing home and us'll get a pair o' sharps putt to 'en, so's us can harness in the hoss.'

'Nonsainse, uncle. You waun' have a bit o' trouble nex' time.'

Wull, he made me try again, and twad'n so turrable bad this time. I got'n in secon' gear, and arter that I putt'n in top gear, and us was flipping along purty middling. I managed to guide'n a bit better, so-long as no other body did'n want none o' the rawd. Us had purt' near two mile o' straight rawd wai'out a corner, and I draived over thik bit o' straight dree or vower times. Of cou'se, the Young Jan would turn 'en around each end, 'cus I had'n hardly come to that pitch o' perfection, not 'eet. But thik turrable sinsation o' being froze beginned to wear off, and Ole Biskit was ready to do more what I wanted for'n to, instaid of amusing hiszel' at my expainse, as you mid say.

'Well, uncle, what's think aw't?' says the boye, nex' time us come to the end o' the straight. 'Have 'ee had nuff? Shall I draive 'ee back 'ome?'

'Old 'ard a minute,' I says, 'I'll jis' take'n vore and back once more. Praps if I was to go careful I might be abble to get'n around the cornders.'

Caw! Didn' he laaf!

'I knows what you'm after,' he says. 'You wants to larn enough so's to be abble to draive back 'ome. Did'n I tell 'ee what 'twould be, arter you'd got over the fus' predicament? Well, come on then. Darn if you shan't swank back home yerzel'.'

Cou'se, I had'n got no sitch thing in me mind.

Still, arter that, I thought I mid-so-well master 'en, now I'd got so fur. And if I *could* draive'n home mezelf, all well and gude. 'Cus the volks sure to rin out to zee, when they yeard the rattle coming.

CHAPTER SEVEN

Through tribulation Jan comes to the state of being able to drive his car along the road without running off the edge or knocking over the milestones.

Wull, I've done it.

I never thought I should, but I can make the Ole Biskit go all by mezel' now. I've done it two-dree times, without any other body titching a thing.

Of cou'se, the Young Jan was close by in case of emergency. But he did'n have to do nothing. I started the ingine, and sot the car gwain, and then made'n stop near about where I wish to. I waun' say that I can choose me awn spot to a ninch, where to finish up. I eetherways goes too fur, or staps a bit short. But that'll come, ar'r a bit.

Mind you, I daun' say I be perfec'. I shouldn' like for you to think that, cus 'twould be telling 'ee a lie. 'Tis a long ways off perfec', and likely to be, too, fer a goodish bit.

And furthermore, I shouldn' like for Ole Biskit to year me say a word that would laid 'n to think that I was the master aw'n. Cus if he was to, I knaw what wude hap'm immejitly. He'd let me zee who was master, in one minute. The very nex' time I ventered to draive 'n he'd push over the pump, or try to squaise his way in the letter-box to the paust office; and then he'd look into the Black Oss fer a drink.

No. I wouldn' say a word to erritate the ole feller, fer worlds.

Still, arter that, I daun' veel so scat now as what I did. 'Tis a bit quare, natterally, arter you've bin doing it all thase years with a pair o' reins, and then come to have a wheel in yer hand, and a passel of levers and pedals in place of a whip. And o' cou'se, the word o' mouth id'n no gude with a car, like 'tis with a hoss, although they tells me I ab'm got out o' the habit of holleying at Ole Biskit when I wants 'n to do anything on the spurt o' the

37

moment. I daun' notice it mezel', but I derzay it sounds a bit quare to other volks.

But 'tis like everything else, I reckon. Practice makes perfec', though 'twill take a doost of a lot o' practice to make me perfec', or even imperfec'.

However, that extry hower that us bide out on the moor made a lot o' difference to me. I got so's I could draive along without rinning off the zides, as the saying is. Mind, I ban't saying I could orwis keep straight. Sometimes 'twould be a near nip fer a vuzbush or a milestoan, but Young Jan would ketch 'n hold quick, and putt'n vitty again. And gradu'ly I got in the way of laiving things alone which did'n belong to me.

When you fus' starts, you'm ap' to twist the ole guiding wheel a bit too aiger, and he turns more than you bargains vor. Well then you tries to putt'n right in a hurry, and bevore you knows where you'm to you'm off the rawd with yer haid where yer tail ought to be. I vound mezel' like that more'n once, and did'n knaw where I was gwain till I got there.

'Guide'n a bit more aisy, uncle,' says the boye. 'Daun' turn 'n so sudden. He'll go straight if you let'n bide.'

Well, then, o' cou'se, the very nex' time us was gwain crooked I thought I'd be a bit more 'gentle and not turn so sharp, and bevore I cude stap the ole toad us was two wheels in the ditch. 'Twas all the wonders in the world us had'n turn tap-an-tail. If Young Jan had'n done something purty quick us would a-bin topsy-turby. Killed, very likely.

"Tis all or nort with me,' I says. 'I'm eetherways too rapid or else I be too laate.'

'You'll be all right in time,' he says.

'I derzay I shall if I lives long 'nuff,' I says. 'But zeeming to me I shall break me neck avore I breaks in this yer 'oss.'

But he only laafed. 'I'll zee you daun' do that,' he says, 'cus I've got a neck as well as you.'

Be-as-twill, arter a bit more practice I got so's I could draive purty middling along the straight. So then I thought I'd like to guide'n around the bend.

And so the next time us come to the end o' the straight I did'n stap, I went around the cornder. Or when I say I went around, I should have went around butiful if it had'n bin fer thik darned ole derecting paust. What fer heaven's sake they putt'n in sitch a

stoobid plaace vor, right bezide the rawd, I can't think. Plainty o'
room fer'n up'n-tap the haidge, and more in the view of
everybody coming both ways. They might have knawed that
anybody would want all the room he could get, turning around
the cornder.

Mind you, I've draived around thik cornder with hoss and trap
hunders o' times, I suppause, and never tooked the laiste notice
aw'n. But hosses ab'm got the same partiality fer derecting
paustis as what moter-cars have. Or I dunnaw if they'm all alike,
but Ole Biskit never can't zee a paust of any kind without
wanting to push 'n over. Gate-paustis and derecting paustis he
can't a-bear, and he'll orwis go out of his way to knack 'em
down, if he gets half a chance.

At laiste, he will when I be draiving aw'n. But when 'tis the
Young Jan he'll turn up his nawse at every paust he zees, and
pass right by within a ninch aw'm, and make wise he never
knawed they was there.

Mind, us did'n knock down the derecting paust. But 'twas near
nip. When I zeed what was coming I did zummat quick with me
hands and veet, and fer once it hap'm to be the right thing. Ole
Biskit stopped daid, a ninch away from 'en. The beggering toad,
he tried his huttermost to shove his nose vore and titch the paust,
but I had the brake on tight, so he had to be satisfied with sniffing
at 'n. But o' cou'se, us couldn' movee.

'Well, what be gwain to do now, uncle?' says the boye.

'Do? Only thing I sees us can do is get out and walk home, and
let the blessid ole car come along when he's hungerd. Unless
Dick Bradferd takes out his axe and cuts down the paust.'

'No call fer that,' he says. 'You let in yer rayverse.'

'Let in who?' I says.

'Let in yer rayverse, and make 'n go back'ards.'

'Gude laur,' I says, 'you daun' want to let in nobody to do that.
Nothing plaises 'n better than to go back'ards, or zideways
eether, fer the matter o' that. Fer two pins he'd rare up on his
hine wheels.'

'Press down the clitch,' he says, 'and push vore the gear lever
so-fur as he'll go. Not the brake! The gear hannle. Now let up the
clitch nice and aisy and us'll go back'ards.'

And I'm jiggered if us did'n. 'Tis wonderful, begad. I suppause
when you let in the rayverse you turns his inzide around so's he

goes oppozyte derection. Be that as it may, when I tooked up me voot us travelled back'ards.

'That'll do,' says the boye. 'Now go vore, and guide'n out in middle o' the rawd.'

And I did, too. And so us got around the cornder. 'Bout o' vive minutes I reckon it took, fust to last, and purt' near cost a new derecting paust, and a new nose for Biskit.

So now us was out on turnpike. 'Tis a middling wide rawd, so-fur as that goes, but there's a bothering high haidge each zide to consider, instead o' the moor to run out upon if necessary. And Ole Biskit zeemed turrable anxious to go picking wile-flowers. If I had'n keep sharp watch on 'en he'd a-bin arter the buttercups and daisies like a shot.

'You'm doing fus' raate, uncle,' says the boye. 'Keep 'en like that.'

'You tell 'en to bide like it. 'Tis him, not me.'

'Rummage. You can make'n do what you like now.'

'Daun' you spaik so loud,' I says, 'else he'll have us in the ditch.'

The boye laafed, but I knowed 'twas true. Us was coming to a sharp bend in the rawd so I beginned to stop 'en.

'Daun' stop,' says Young Jan. 'Jis' guide'n the laistest bit and he'll go around lovely.'

I ought to have stopped, railly, same's I intainded, but I was sort-of in two minds like, and before I could choose between the two, us was right up home to the bend, and flipping along like the weend. Or so it zeemed to me, although the Young Jan said us wad'n gwain no more'n a hoss's trot. I could veel my hair an' whiskers sticking out like a packet o' peens, and Ole Biskit beginned to look about fer a paust of some sort.

'What do I do now?' I 'olleyed.

'Jis' guide'n around gentle. You'll be all right.'

Wull, how it comes about I dunnaw. Whether I hapm'd to turn 'en jis' the right amount; or whether Biskit did'n see nothing that took his vancy, I can't tell 'ee. Be-as-twill, us went around without a 'itch, and I was jis' gwain to let out the breath what I'd bin holding, and take in a fresh lot, when what should I zee but a hoss and cart, not a gun-shot away and coming right towards us. He looked as big as a houze, and there did'n zeem room to push a wheelbarra past, never mind a moter-car.

40

Caw, my dear zaul! I went jis like a piece o' stone all over. And 'twas a gude job I did, fer if I'd had the power to move I'd a-done zummat with thik guiding wheel, gudeness knaws what, and in one minute us would have been up over the haidge, lock, stock an' barreel.

'Keep 'n straight, uncle,' says the boye.

'Us can't get by. There id'n room,' I holleyed.

'There's hunderds o' room,' he says. 'Keep on as you be.'

I couldn' do no other, cus me sainses had all lef' me. I couldn' zee how 'twas possible fer they two vayacles to pass one-'tother without a calamity. Biskit dashed at the hoss and cart like a thinder-bolt. Or so it zeemed to me. I could zee everything and everybody smaished all abroad to hattoms. And the next minute I zeed the hoss and cart go past. How it hapm'd I dunnaw, ner I can't think.

And although 'twas only fer a flash, as you mind say, 'twas wonderful what I noticed gwain by. I zeed 'twas buttcher Parks's cart, and Josep' Parks was draiving. And I yeard'n say 'Jan,' and I said 'Josep'.' And with the zame us was past. And us never titched. Us passed and never titched. I couldn' believe 'twas true, cus I was waiting fer the crash. And I veeled me hat coming back on to me haid, and me cloas titching me body again, as the hairs lied down what had been stood up straight. And the Young Jan remarked, 'Who said he cude'n draive!'

And I knowed as well as I knowed me awn name that Josep' Parks was turned around in his sate looking arter me with his mouthe wide ope', and the eyes aw'n jumping out of his haid. I'd a-give zummat to be abble to turn round to zee, but I had'n hardly come to that, not 'eet.

And then us come vore to Orcombe Cross which was the wist cornder o' the lot. But zummat come over me so's I steered around the bend without a ninch eether way. So then us was on the straight fer Muddlecombe village, and I zeed the Young Jan out o' the cornder of me eye take out his pipe and start to full 'en up with baccy.

And I zeed a moter-car as big as a church, or thereabouts, coming up the rawd. 'Twas only li'l narrer rawd this time, not the turnpike. But I said to mezel', 'What is to be will be,' and I kept right ahaid, and next minute us flipped past one-t'other and never titched. And I heard the Young Jan laaf to hizel', and he stoopied down and lighted up his ole pipe.

Another couple o' minutes and us was in zight o' the houze. I wanted most turrable to blow up the ole hooter, cus it did zeem a pity fer me to go draiving the car right up to the door, or thereabouts, and nobody to witness it. But to blow the hooter meaned taking one hand away from the guiding wheel, and I couldn' bring mezel' to take sitch a risk. I was itching to do it, but I did'n know what capers Ole Biskit might get up to if he was to come to know that I was only controlling of 'n with me left hand. And o' cou'se, if I was to blow the hooter he'd be aware in a minute that I'd only got one hand to the wheel. I knows you'm thinking that 'twas stoobid of me to imagine that the ole car cude tell what was gwain on. But you go an' draive one fer the fus' time, and zee if you waun' get the zame idaya in yer haid. You'll have the veeling all the time that he'm watching of 'ee out o' the cornder of his eye. You'll be very different to me if you daun't.

And while all this was gwain through me mind the boye said, 'Blow yer horn, uncle.'

Will it be all right?'

'All right? Yes.'

So I took me hand away quick and give the ole bladder a squaise. And I spause, in me hurry, like, I squaise 'n purty hard, and I'm blest if I did'n frighten mezel'. 'Twas zacly same as if the ole cow had belved right in me yer-awl. Properly made me jump, and I suppose with the shock I give a kick to the acsillyrater, and darned if Ole Biskit did'n jump too. Fer a minute I thought I'd upzet his applecart, but I managed to keep'n out o' mischief, and us stayed on the rawd.

Luckily, mother and the maid yeard the zound o' the horn, and they come rishing out to the gate jist in time to zee me coming up the straight. Young Jan waved up his 'at, and I yeard Jane holley, "Tis vather draiving.'

'Now,' I thought to mezel', 'if only I can manage to stop somewhere about the right plaace, 'twill open their eyes.'

And darn 'ee I wad'n more 'n a lan'-yard out. I did'n get in very close to the side, I'll admit, and I left the car a bit on the skew-wiff, but that wad'n no gurt criterion. I'd brought 'n 'ome, which nobody couldn' deny. Cus there was the car, still in working order, and there was me alive and well. And nobody more surprised than myself.

42

CHAPTER EIGHT

Jan causes a death.

They all said my draiving Ole Biskit would be the death o' zomebody, and I'm vexed to zay it have come true in a sort of a way. I suppause zome day I shall year the last aw't, but it waunt be yet-a-bit fer certin.

Us was returning back from Barleycombe, me and mother, the Young Jan and my darter Jane. Young Jan said I mus' draive, cus I'd got on very well, and had'n got nothing to fear. Mother wad'n so aiger.

'Tid'n what *he've* got to fear,' her says, ''tis what the rest of us has got to fear.'

'That's all right, aunt,' says the boye. 'Uncle's as safe as a church.'

'I don't mind the church. 'Tis the churchyard I'm thinking about,' her says.

I did'n pay no 'tention to that, 'cus I did'n think it worth-a-while. 'Tis jis the soort o' remark her *would* make. But 'tis a pity anything should have hap'm'd amiss, cus it give her the chance to say, 'There, did'n I zay zo!' And there's nothing delights mother more than to be abble to say, 'There, what did I tell 'ee?'

'Twas a zimple li'l thing too. If it had hapm'd to any other body nothing wouldn't have been said about it, 'sep to laaf at it. But becus it hapm'd to be poor ole Jan Stewer everybody mus' make a song about it.

'I'd bin doing very well, too, considering. All out through Barleycombe Vore Strate, and down along Mill Rawd, I never pushed into a thing, and never scat nothing over. And I turned around the cornder by the clock, all by mezel', and never so-much as titched the lamp-paust sticked right up in the middle o' the rawd.

Zo I beginned to think I railly was coming to it, as the saying is. The furder I went the more confidence I got. An' confidence is half the battle in matters o' that soort. That's all you wants, is confidence, and I could veel it coming over me. Why, bless yer zaul, I even got so fur as to start talking while I was draiving. But mother very zoon told me to stop yapping, and keep me mind on what I was doing.

Wull, and o' cou'se, jis as I was getting on very nice, and everything gwain along cabbical, and me thinking that I was getting past me troubles, and looking vorward to the time when I should be abble to take away one hand from the guiding wheel and titch me hat to the volks gwain by, this-yer blimming accident mus' come along and upzet the whole applecart, as the saying is.

'Twas on the straight bit o' rawd from Two Mile Stone to Week Cross. That's where it hapm'd to. O' cou'se, you can zee right ahaid of 'ee fer upperds of a mile, and Tom Dergis plaace is zacly half-ways in the middle. Wull, Tom was one o' the very men that I thought I should like to witness me driving a car in a proper manner, cus he'm one o' they what be orwis ready to laaf at other volks, and make out they ab'm got no more sainse than what he have hiszel', which id'n very much. And Tom Dergis had said one or two things about me and Ole Biskit which I wad'n very much enamoured of.

Wull, I could zee there wad'n no obstacle in the way, and no other vayacle wanting to pass, so I thought to mezel', 'I'll jis flip along yer a bit smart like, and let Maister Tom zee that I ban't so wanting as he thinks I be.'

Zo I putt me voot on the acsillyrater. Ole Biskit pricked up his yers, and away-do-go like a burd flying. The Young Jan seed what I was on upon. 'That's right, uncle,' he says. 'Let 'n lick a bit. 'Tis safe as eggs, vore yer.'

I be dalled if us wad'n gwain along like one train. The haidges was properly flipping by. Mother sot up and opened her eyes. 'Yer, stiddy on, mump'aid,' her says. 'Not so vast. What be thinking about?' But I putt me voot down a bit harder, and o' cou'se that made 'n go quicker again. Flying over the ground, us was. That's what us was, properly flying. You couldn' call it no other.

'If you daun' go a bit more aisy, my vine veller,' says Ann, 'I'll give you a scat across the haid with my anbrella.'

'Let'n alone, mother,' says Jane. ''Tis all right.'

''Tis all right while *'tis* all right,' her says, 'and when tid'n all right 'twill be all wrong.'

However. Us was trav'ling vore to Tom's plaace hunderd mile a nower, I should think, and I was jis' wishing the ole feller was there to zee me draive past, when I'm pippered if he did'n stap out from his gate into the rawd. Couldn' have hapm'd better.

My blessid! 'Toot, toot,' I goes on the ole hooter to make 'n look around, and when he railised who was draiving I shall never ferget the look that come over his faace. Properly tooked his breath away. All he could do was to stand there gap-mouthid.

Dear me, I wished with all me 'art that I could look around and shake up one hand to 'en, gwain past, jis' to let'n zee that I was properly proficient. But I had'n come to that state o' perfection, not hardly. I had to ketch the wheel hold tight, and keep me eyes fixed where I was gwain, else I knowed I should go somewhere differnt. But I holleyed out, 'Gude aiv'min, Tom,' in the most ord'nery voice I cude manage.

Everything was gwain cabbical, jist as I ordained for it to. In me mind I could zee ole Tom Dergis rishing up to the Black Oss and telling about how he'd glimpsed Jan Stewer draiving a moter-car like's if he'd bin accustomed to it ever since he was born. And I could yer the t'others say, 'Ees, the ole Jan id'n sitch a fule as he looks.'

And then, I be dalled, jis' as I was veeling nice and plaised with mezel', and thinking how well everything was gwain on, that blimming ole hen mus' come out and upzet the whole contrac'.

How is it that zummat must orwis crop up like that to spoil the effec', jist when you laistest wants it to?

Where her come from I dunnaw. One o' Tom's hens 'twas, o' cou'se. Lied up in haidge I spause her was, and frightened out by Ole Biskit's racket. Be that as it may, her appeared all-to-once, right in middle o' the rawd. I did'n have time to do nothing. I did'n have time to spaik. I did'n have time to thin. Fus' thing I knawed, her was right in front o' me wheels. In one minute all me confidence was gone scat. I zeemed to go quatt, zacly like one o' they balloon things arter zomebody have sticked a peen in 'en. Me wits flied up into me 'at. Me eyes jumped out o' me haid. I went goozey all over. I lost all account of levers an' hannles, acsillyrater and all the rest aw't. Like a fule I lained out over the zide and holleyed to the vowel, top o' me voice. What I said to her I dunnaw, but whatever 'twas, 'twas too laate.

Wull, o' cou'se, me jumping like that, twested the ole guiding wheel all over one zide, and what hapm'd arter that I can't tell 'ee.

Natterally, the raate us was gwain sent the whole contraption flying towards the bank. The hen her squawked. Mother her holleyed. Jane her squailed. Tom Dergis he swared. The boye he shouted. As fer me, I shut me eyes and waited fer the car to strike the bank and send us all to kingdom come. Bu zacly as us was gwain slap-bang into distruction the Young Jan jumped to the wheel, fetched Ole Biskit around straight and brought'n to a stan still.

So everybody was abble to breathe again, 'sep the ole hen. Her breathing days was over. I'd killed her, daid as mutton.

And then us had to harken to Tom fer a bit. What he said wad'n a scrap like I'd bin looking vorrad to. He had'n got a word to say in praise of my draiving. Matter o' fac' 'twas zacly oppozyte. Nothing wad'n bad nuff for it. 'Twas people like me, he said, what brought jidgments on the land. 'Twas time the government putt a stop, he said, to volks dashing about in moter-cars when they had'n got sufficient sainse to push along a weelbarra. There was a proper place fer people what was mazed, he said, and that was the lunatic 'zylum, not the turnpike. There ought to be a law made, he reckoned that any man could be intitled to take a gun and shoot the volks what went coosing about the faace of the earth, zeeking who they mid devour. He'd zummons me right up bevore the jidge, he said, and have no putt into prisin, and then he'd zee whether I'd go raging and tearing about distroying other volk's property.

And as fer Tom's hen, you'd a-thought 'twas the only thing he'd got in the world to live for. Best hen in parrish, laid zix aigs a wik, and never knawed to hatch less 'n leb'm chicks out of a sittin', and orwis more'n half pullets.

Cou'se, 'twas all lies, you mid depaind. I derzay 'twas the wist hen he'd got. But there 'twas. I'd a-killed 'n, and I had to recompense the ole feller twice over. And I give n another shulling 'pon-tap o' that not to zay a word to nobody.

And a vat lot o' gude that was. Fer that-there blimming ole Lias Buzzacott was up in Tom's ricksplat and witnessed the whole cantastrophy. And bevore us got home, the news was all over the parrish.

46

CHAPTER NINE

Jan is persuaded that Biskit knows when to play his tricks.

Nobody won't make me believe that the Ole Biskit id'n capable
of knowing when I be draiving on me awn risponsibility. What I
mean to say, when the Young Jan id'n there bezide me in case
zummat should go wrong. He knaws so-well as what I do, and 'tis
no gude to tell me differnt. I dunnaw where he keeps his eyes to.
I wish I did, begad. I'd bline-mop the ole toad, I would.

Ees, bless yer 'art, he knawth when 'tis only me out with 'n.
Else why should he orwis choose they journeys to play up his ole
pranks? Tid'n to say 'tis aught to do with the draiving, 'cus
zometimes I shall go a whole long journey with the Young Jan
sot up bezide me, and the boye shan't turn his hand upzide-
down. I shall do every mortle thing mezel'. I shall manoover all
the hannles about, an' manipilate the acsillyrater, and work the
gears, and blow the hooter, all according to the derections on the
bottle, as the saying is. And nothing shan't go wrong. I shall go
up-'eel and down dale, around the cornders and in an' out
amongs' the travvic, and Ole Biskit shall do his work like a chap
what is being paid by the job. And the Young Jan shall say, 'I'm
jiggered if you ab'm mastered it now, uncle. You ab'm got
nothing more to be feared about. You'm abble to draive so-well
as the next.'

But I knaws very well all the time, that 'tis only cus he'm riding
with me. Ole Biskit is aware that if aught goes wrong Young Jan
can putt it right in a jiffy, and so tid'n worth-a-while. But you let
me go draiving by mezel', when the boye id'n there, and I'll
make a bet he'll play up every caper imaginable. He jis' delights
to get his works tied up in a knot, cus he knaws I can't undo 'em.

And the beggering toad, he'll take jolly gude care not to do it
when there's anybody to lend a feller a hand. Not he! He'll wait
till he've got me out in zome lonely ole spot, hunderd mile from

47

nowhere, where there id'n likely to be a soul pass by fer howers, and then he'll get zome complaint in his inzide which he knaws very well I can't remedy. Praps 'twill be the 'iccups so's he can only go along by jits an' starts, or else he'll get a nasty cough and spit as if he was gone in the weend. And zometimes he'll jib altogether and turn properly sulky, so's you can't move 'n vore ner back. And 'tis only cus he knaws I ab'm got the gumtion to do the right thing to make 'n go proper.

I tell 'ee zometimes I gets that wicked I veels like's if I cude give'n a gude kick. Cus I knaws he'm only laafing at me.

Wull, I'll tell 'ee a li'l caper I had with 'n t'other day, and then you say whether he daun' know when 'tis best time to play up his ole tricks.

Ned Annaferd and Lias Buzzacott was both telling about gwain over to the sale to Buck's Barton. And I wanted to go over so-far mezel', cus there was one or two things there which I shouldn' mind bidding for if they was gwain to be gived away. So I said I'd do 'em a kindness and take 'em over in the car, cus I thought that they two and me and the Young Jan wude make up a party, zacly. Wull, they said they'd be very welcome, cus 'tis a matter o' nine-tain mile to Buck's Barton, and all-so-fur back again; or a bit furder, cuz 'tis mostly up-'eel.

That was all well and gude. But when the day come, the Young Jan found he wad'n abble to go, cus he had zummat else which mus' be 'tended to. That was a nasty scat fer me, cus I'd bin depending on he in case Ole Biskit shude start any of his ole crams. And I did'n like to run word with Ned and Lias arter promising they should go.

'You'll be all right, uncle,' says the boye. ''Twill be nice li'l draive fer 'ee, and gude rawd all the way,'

I fancied Ned and Lias looked down over their noses a bit when I went along with the car and they found the boye wad'n gwain. I dersay they wouldn' a-bin so aiger if they'd knawed that in the fus' plaace.

'I spause you'm capable, Jan?' says Ned.

'Caw, darn 'ee,' I says. 'What do 'ee mean, capable! I've drove scores o' miles.'

'But you ab'm had sitch valu'ble passengers as you got now,' says Lias.

'Aw, ab'm I! What about las' wik when I tooked a couple o' calves into Kirton market?'

48

However. Us started off all right, and half the parrish was there to zee us go. Everything went nice and suant fer the fus' vew miles. Ole Biskit behaved hiszel' like a zindy-skule taicher having tay at the parsonidge. You couldn' wish for better manners.

'Well, what about capable now, then?' I says.

'I'm darned if you ab'm got the nick aw't, Jan,' says Ned. 'Do's it very well, daun' he, Lias?'

'Wonderful,' says Lias. 'I didn't think he'd got the brains.'

Wull, us went on very nice till us got out middle o' the moor. And then, all-to-once, I beginned to raillise that Ole Biskit was up to one of his li'l capers again. 'Twas a fresh gyte thees time. Zummat which I never had'n experienced bevore. 'Twad'n very much at first, only he was trying his hardest all the time to be gwain over to one zide the rawd, instead o' keeping straight. That wad'n nothing new, o'cou'se, but orwis bevore, when he wanted to do that he'd do it all in one go, wai'out stopping to think. Thees time 'twas only gradule, a bit to a time. I could veel 'en pulling and pulling to the off, and I had to push the guiding wheel hard the oppozyte way to keep 'n in the middle o' the rawd. Ord'nery times he'd go along straight of his awn accord, and you only want to keep the wheel stiddy. But now I'd got the works o' the world to keep 'n from rinning into the ditch.

And the vurder us waint, the harder he was pulling to the right, till I'd got all I could do to keep his nawse the way us wanted to go. If I let'n have his haid fer one second he'd be off to the haidge-traw like a rabbut. 'Twas a turrable unconferable sinsation, and I was sw'atting strames. I durzen go more'n a walking paze feared I wouldn' be abble to keep 'en out from the ditch. But I did'n say nothing, cus I thought praps he'd come to his sainses in a minute, and go along in a proper manner. But 'twas mortle hard work, and o' cou'se, a feller was worritting all the time, wondering whatever could be the cause of it.

And sometimes he'd nearly get the better of me, and then I'd give the ole guiding wheel a twest the other way and us would shoot right across the rawd. Then they two would holley out, 'Woop,' and 'Take care, Jan,' and ketch hold to the side.

And instaid o' getting better he got wiss, so that to-last I'd got so-much as ever I could do to keep 'n on the rawd at all.

49

'Whatever be 'bout of, Jan?' says Ned. 'You'm womm'ling one-zide and t'other as if you was gwain home from the rent-audit dinner. Why daun' 'ee keep 'n straight?'

So then I was forced to tell 'em.

'I can't,' I says. 'The ole toad's all the time trying to turn into the haidge.'

'Wull, daun' 'ee let'n to, fer heab'm's sake,' says Ned.

'Why did'n 'ee give 'n a feed o' grass bevore you took 'n out if that's what he wants?' says Lias.

Jus' then I had to turn a bit to the right to go around the bend, and I twisted the guiding wheel what I thought was the proper amount. But Ole Biskit he added a lot more on to it, and I'm blowed if he did'n flick his haid around, and bevore I could do aught to stap'n he'd got one wheel in the ditch. I putt on the brake jist in time. Nex' minute he'd a-bin over the haidge into a vield o' turmits.

'Aw, I zee,' says Lias, "tis roots he'm after.'

But I wad'n in no mood fer joking, and Ned wad'n, nuther, cus us might jis-so-well bin turned over and killed, as not.

And there I was in the zame ole quandairy again. Miles from anywhere and Ole Biskit lied up in the haidge.

'What do us do now?' says Lias. 'Go picking flowers, I spause.'

'Let's look and zee what's the matter with the stoobid toad,' I says.

So us all lookid at 'n, hard. But us wad'n no wiser than us was bevore.

'Do 'ee think it can be indisgestion, Jan?' says Lias. 'How do 'ee make 'n putt out his tongue?'

'If us was to push 'n back on the rawd,' says Ned, 'us could zee right around 'n.'

'If us was to turn 'n upzide down,' says Lias, 'us could zee in under. But I dunnaw what gude it would be.'

Hold thee baal, mump'aid,' says Ned, 'and come yer and push.'

'Be us gwain to push 'n all the way to Buck's Barton?' says Lias. 'Cus the zale's to-day, 's-knaw, not nex' wik.'

However, us got'n back on the rawd arter a lot o' shoving, and then us walked around, all dree of us. Lias went in front and said he was the band, and made wise to play the trambone. Cou'se, he can't help o' being fulish. 'Tis natteral with 'n. But us did'n vind out what was the matter.

50

Then Lias said us ought to turn about and march back the other way round, cus the view wude be differnt on the return journey. And I'm blawed if he did'n too, mimmicking up his ole muzic, like zome skule-cheel.

'Muzzen take no notice o' Lias,' says Ned. 'He id'n accountable fer his actions.'

All-to-once Lias stops.

'Did this weel ought to be like this-yer, Jan?' he says.

'What is he, round instead o' square?' says Ned.

'Looks to me,' he says, 'more like as if he was square instead o' round. He'm vlat as a pancake. You got a pumsher, Jan, that's what you got.'

And I'm jiggered if he wad'n right. The off vore weel was resting down on the timbern part.

'Did'n I tell 'ee us would get a better view gwain back?' says Lias. 'You wouldn' harken to me.'

''Tis what have made Ole Biskit pull to the off, you mid depend, Jan,' says Ned. 'That accounts fer't.'

'Poor feller was out o' weend,' says Lias. 'You made'n go too vast, Jan, and he've lost his breath. Let'n bide and blaw a bit and his tyre will full up again, I daresay.'

'I wish he'd got some o the weend that you'm wasting so much,' I says.

'What be us gwain to do now?' says Ned. 'Can you putt'n to rights, Jan?'

'I dunnaw that I can mend 'en, Ned,' I says. 'But there's a odd weel yer that us could putt on in plaace aw'n if us knawed the way.'

'Us could putt wings on 'en and fly if us knawed the way,' says Lias.

'Caw, darn 'ee,' says Ned, 'if a weel-wright can't putt on a weel 'tis a poor come-along-of-it. I've putt weels on half the vayacles in the parrish, although none aw'm wad'n moters. What tools have 'ee got?'

'There's a box-vull yer,' I says, 'but I dunnaw what they'm vor. You 'elp yerzel'.'

'If there's a cork-screw amongst 'em,' says Lias, 'I could show 'ee how to use that if you lend me a bottle o' beer.'

However. Ned had a gude look to the weels to zee how they did fit, and I'm blawed if he did'n vind out the way aw't, arter he'd stiddid 'em fer a bit. He tooked off the old one and putt on the fresh one in the plaace aw't. I was a trifle anxious when it come to draiving, feared he wad'n on proper. But he was all right, zeem-zo.

Lias watched out over the zide fer a bit to make sure he was gwain viddy. 'If you zee 'en wommle,' I says, 'you holley to me to stap.'

'I daresay I shall,' he says.

However, he did'n wommle. 'He'm doing splendid,' says Lias. 'He'm gwain around almost so-vast as the rest, although he ab'm had half the experience.'

But us had lost so much time on the rawd that when us got to Buck's Barton us meet the volks coming away from the zale. And o' cou'se us larned that the things had gone durt chaip.

'I'm vezed, sure nuff, Ned,' I says. ''Tis orwis like it. The blimming ole toad wude'n a-thought o' doing such a thing if the Young Jan had bin presint.'

'Aw, come now, Jan,' he says. 'Muzzen blame Ole Biskit fer a pumsher. Mid-so-well blame the hoss fer picking up a stoan.'

But there 'tis. Orwis the zame.

Ole Biskit knaw'th. He knaw'th, I tell 'ee, and nothing waunt make me believe no other.

CHAPTER TEN

Jan takes a party for a day's outing and wishes he had thought twice before starting.

'Tis a wonder I be alive to tell the tale, 'pon me zaul. If I'd knowed what I was gwain through I'd a-drownded mezel' fust. But I did'n know, and there wad'n nobody to tell me.

Mrs. Snell started the idaya, quite innocent like. Her hap'm to pass along when I was washing a bit of the muck off Ole Biskit and shining up the brass.

'When be gwain to take me fer a ride, maister?' her said.

'Any time you mind to name, Mrs. Snell,' I says. 'I'll draive 'ee home now, if you say the word.'

'Aw, I daun' mean a li'l fiddling ride like that,' her saith. 'I means a proper long journey to some plaace where I wouldn' go else.'

So then my missis cheemed in. 'Caw, bless yer zaul, Mrs. Snell,' her said, *'he'd* never take 'ee no-plaace. He daun' even take me, let alone any other body. So-fur as riding fer pleasure is consarned us mid-so-well have a dree-weel-butt about the plaace as thik ole thing. 'Tis neether ornament ner use.'

'Daun' 'ee tell up sitch falsehudes,' I says. 'You never wants to ride no-place, that's what's the matter.'

'Aw, daun' I?' her saith. 'There's heaps o' plaaces I'd like to go to, if I had the chance.'

'Well, name one then,' I says, 'and I'll take 'ee there like a shot.'

Wull, one word led to another, and Mrs. Snell said her'd yeard a lot about Lynton, and never been there, but some relations of hers had spent 'ollerdy there, and they come back full aw't.

'But I reckon that would be too fur fer Ole Biskit,' her says. 'although they draived from all down Plymouth and back in a moter. But I spause he was more up-to-daate, like.'

53

Wull, nobody daun' like to yer things like that said about his moter-car, so I up and told her purty quick that Biskit would go wherever any other car would, never mind about up-to-daate, or down-to-daate.

So the upshot o' that was, 'twas decided us would go fer trip to Lynton fer the day. If they'd said Timbuctoo I'd have took 'em on, arter running down Ole Biskit, with their 'up-to-daate.'

But mind you, I was depainding on the Young Jan gwain along too, and when he said he wouldn' be abble to go, I wished I had'n bin hardly zo vast. I couldn' very well get out aw't now, and they invited Mrs. Endycott to make up the vower. Her jumped to the chance, cus there wad'n nothing to pay.

'Twas ordained to go the volleying Zaturdy, and the women-volk prepared all manner o' things to ait an' drink. You'd a-thought us was gwain on a desert island to live fer a vortnit, to zee what quantities they did take along. And the Young Jan had a gude look to Ole Biskit, to zee that his innerds was all right, and a-plenty o' petrol an' oil, and all sitch like.

Zo us started off as big as life fus' thing Zaturday morning, me and mother in front and Mrs. Snell and Mrs. Endycott behind. I tried hard fer mother to zit behind in exchange fer one o' the t'others, but couldn' get her to. Her reckons her can help me with the draiving if her's sot up beside me, but her's a sight more hinedrance than help. Her do keep on to anybody zo. This is mother all the way:

'Mind, you'm in too close this side. Keep over a bit, you'll have us in the ditch in a minute. Look out, stoobid, there's a car coming. Pull in a bit. Go out a bit. Take care what you'm doing. Why daun' you look where you'm gwain? You very nearly had collision that time. Mind this-yer dog, and not go so reckless. That id'n the way to go around a cornder. You'll have the ole thing tap-an-tail in a minute.'

That's how her go'th on all the time, and sometimes it makes anybody say things he did'n ought to. Cou'se her daun' mean nothing by it. 'Tis over-anxiousness.

However. Us went all right to Barnstable. Ole Biskit behaved hiszel' butiful. Went along so-suant as a train, he did. Never jibbed, ner shied, ner nort. I yerd Mrs. Snell say all manner o' nice things about my draiving. But I thought to mezel', 'There's heaps o' time yet.'

I guided the car all up droo Barnstable strate without scatting aught, more'n jis pushing one chap up on the path; but that was proper place for 'en; and then us enquired the way to Lynton. When us got a bit vurder on the rawd the women-volk considered 'twas time us had a bit o' summat to ait, so us pulled in bezide the hedge and had our vorenoons. And a proper merry party us was too, I can assure 'ee.

But when us come to start again, I be dalled if the merriment did'n soon come to end. Think I cude make the ole begger go? I turned around thik starting hannle till I was black in the faace. But Ole Biskit did'n take no more notice than if I'd bin turning the mangle.

And mind you, I dunnaw whether you've ever tried turning around one o' they starting hannles or no, but if you keeps it up long nuff I'm jiggered if it won't make 'ee sw'at. And looked to me like's if I might keep it up all day an' all night. O' cou'se, like everything else, there's a nick in it. I can manage it arter a fashion when he'm in a gude timper and liable to start middling aisy. But when he'm pig-haided and not in the mood for it, 'tis a buster. But I never knawed 'en so contr'y as he was tho.

I could turn and turn till me eyes was dropping out, and soon's I stopped, he'd stop. And o' cou'se, jis when anybody was turrified to death, and raddy to kick the whole contraption all to flibbits one o' they women-volk would come out with some stoobid remark that made 'ee go preckles all over.

Arter I'd had another go at'n, and turned the hannle round till all the breath was gone out o' me body, ole Mother Endycott would say, 'Waun' he go, Jan?'

Caw, I tell 'ee, 'twas mortle hard to spaik civil when you was half daid and the arms of 'ee purt' near tore out o' their sockets, and then fer zombody to ax 'ee if he wouldn' go.

'I dersay he'd go if us was to push 'n,' I said.

Then Mrs. Snell cheems in. 'I spause you'm turning aw'n the right way, Jan? Would he start better, do 'ee think, if you was to wind 'n oppozyte derection?'

'You can't be doing the right thing, for certin,' says Mrs. Endycott, 'cus he wouldn' bring us all this way and then go wrong all-to-once.'

Then they'd go poking all around to zee if they could discover what was wrong. And every wips-wile one aw'm would say. 'It mus' be something.' If they said that once they said it vifty times.

And every time they come around where I was to they'd tell me what they'd thought might be the matter since they was round last. Mrs. Endycott said, 'Is it aught to do with the stame, Jan, do 'ee think? I remember once when the injine couldn' pull up the steepy bit to Week Tunnel they reckoned 'twas becus he'd rinned out o' stame.'

'I've got all the stame I wants, missis,' I says.

'I daun' vancy you've got a turrable lot o' wind in the wheels,' says Mrs. Snell. 'Praps 'tis that what's doing it.'

'And there's plenty nuff wind, missis,' I says, although my meaning was differnt to what hers was.

Then mother noticed that one o' the lamps wad'n properly upright. So her putt'n straight, and then her told me to try'n again, and zee if he'd go better now.

'Daun' be so sauft,' I says. 'How do 'ee think the lamps could have aught to do with it?'

'You never know,' her says. 'You can't vind out what's the matter. Why shouldn' I?'

But nothing us could do wouldn' make'n go, and there us was, miles away from everywhere, and there us was likely to bide. Mrs. Snell was the only one what did'n sim to trouble about it, and the wiss-tempered I got, the more her did laaf.

'What odds?' her saith. 'Us have got a-plenty to ait and a-plenty to drink. Let the ole mump'aid bide till he gets tired o' standing and then he'll go off of his awn accord.'

However. Arter a bit another moter-car come along, and the gen'lman stopped and axed if there was aught the matter.

'I dunnaw,' I says. 'I can't get the ole toad to start.'

So he got out and turned around the hannle fer a bit, but Ole Biskit wouldn' do no more fer he than what he did fer me.

'Have 'ee got petrol?' he says.

'Ees,' I says. 'Nuff to drown 'en.'

'Is 'er swished on?'

Caw! Darn my riggs. I never could mind that ole swishing business. But soon's ever the gen'lman mentioned the word I knowed what was the matter in a minute. You pushes up the ole swish when you staps, and you mus' push 'n down again avore you starts. What gude it do's I dunnaw, but Ole Biskit knows in a minute if 'tis pointing the wrong way, and he won't budge till 'tis putt right. I've told 'ee before what a pecooliar chap he is, and that's one of his ole crams. I jis putt me vinger to the swish, and then one turn to the hannle, and away-do-go.

My gudeness gracious. All that scummer over a li'l thing like that.

Ees. And then to cap the lot, my Ann says, 'I've bin looking to thikky thing ever so many times, and I was jis gwain to ax 'ee if he did'n ought to be pointing t'other way. I thought that was the cause aw't, but, I did'n say so, cus you only poo-poo's it when I say anything.'

That's the soort o' thing a man must expec' if he takes out a passel o' women-volk.

However. Us got moving again. But whether Ole Biskit had got annoyed with the things I'd said about 'n while I was turning around thik blessid hannle, or whether he'd come to the end of his gude behaviour, I can't tell 'ee. Be-as-twill, from that time onward he wad'n like the zame car. He went right into one of his contr'y moods again. 'Twas jis' like as if he thought to hiszel', 'I've got ole Jan Stewer miles away from everywhere and now I'll play 'en up a nice ole caper.'

'Twad'n to say that he jibbed, exac'ly. He did'n acsh'ly refuse to go. In fac', zometimes he'd rin along nice fer a mile or two and I'd think it had got right again. And then, all-to-once, he'd go all umpy-jumpy in his inzide, and get so waik as a robin. Speshly if 'twas a bit agin 'eel. Laistest bit o' collerwork and he'd puff an blaw like a broken-winded hoss. I'd have the works o' the world to make'n reach the top.

And, by jo, 'tis 'eels out in that distric'! There id'n nuff flat contry to play skiddles. If you ban't gwain up one zide of a houze you'm gwain down t'other.

Not but what Ole Biskit would go down-'eel all right. Matter o' fac', he'd go down-over a bit too quick for my liking, and I was forced to putt on they brakes middling hard to keep 'n back. And the vurder us went the more steepy the 'eels did become. I tell 'ee straight, they got like that to-last, that I did'n very much like the look aw'm, not being accustomed to it, as you might say.

'Us be getting up in the mountaineous country I should think,' I says.

'I spause you can hold'n back all right, gwain down over, can't 'ee, Jan?' says Mrs. Endycott.

'Wull, I 'ope I shall, missis,' I says, 'but I zeem he takes a doost of a lot o' restraining.'

Caw! My blassid! I s'pause I ought to 'a-said it differnt to that, but 'twas what was in me mind, and what's 'pon-tap boils out over fust. But I'm blawed if I did'n have a proper barney with they women-volk arter that. Speshly Mrs. Endycott. Every time us went down over a bit of a nap her was up and down like a Punch and Judy shaw.

'Take care, Jan. This is a nasty 'eel. Putt the brake on hard, cheel. 'Tis turrable steepy. You'm gwain too vast, I tell 'ee. You waun' be abble to stap 'n, I'm sure you waunt. Stiddy! You'll never get around the bend, never in this world. If there's ort coming around the cornder us'll go scat right into 'en. Can't 'elp aw't. Us'll be scat all to flibbits.'

And zo her'd keep on. 'Why daun' 'ee let the poor man alone?' says Mrs. Snell.

'All very well,' her says. 'S'pause the blessid thing was to turn over. Where should us be to, then?'

'Upzide down,' says Mrs. Snell.

But all zame, I mus' confess I wad'n veeling properly comferable, and I wished with all me 'art that the Young Jan was there, cus I knawed very well that Ole Biskit wad'n right. Every time us come to the laistest bit of a 'eel he'd puff an' blaw, and go faint, and start sorter logging in his inzide.

'What makes 'n keep jerking zo, Jan?' says Mrs. Snell.

Zo I said zame as Young Jan said once bevore when he was behaving zummat similar.

'I think the ingine is missing,' I says.

'Aw, that's bad,' her says. 'Sure you had'n when us started?'

'Had what?' I says.

'Why, the ingine. I'd a-thought us would a-noticed if he'd valled off gwain along. When did you fust miss 'en?'

What could anybody say to that?

However. Us managed to scrall along some way or 'nother till us come to a plaace caaled Parracombe, and then us had to go down sitch a 'eel as I'd never zeed bevore in me life. When us turned around the bend and I zeed what us had got to go down over, I tell 'ee straight I was properly vrightened.

'You better-way stop,' my wive said. 'Us'll get out and walk down over yer.'

58

'No gude you telling about stopping,' I says. 'If he stops now 'twill be of his awn accord. You'll have to bide till us gets to the bottom, if us ever do get there.'

Caw, dally! Mrs. Endycott yeard what I said and I thought her would certinly jump out over the zide. However, there did'n hap'm to be nothing in the way, and us got down bottom right zide up.

And then us had jis sitch another 'eel to go up t'other zide. I knawed Ole Biskit wude'n do it the minute I looked up and zeed where us had to go to. 'Twas jis like gwain up the zide of a houze, and us had'n got very fur bevore Ole Biskit gived up the goast. I veeled he was gwain to stap, and I was feared o' me life that he'd take and rin back-erds, and dash us all to hattoms down bottom. However, I managed to guide'n into the zide, and there us sticked with the hine wheels in the ditch.

My dear zaul. If they women wad'n out in the rawd avore you could say 'knive.' You'd never think they could be zo dapper to look at 'em.

'What be us gwain to do now?' says Mrs. Snell.

'Trapes back 'ome again, I reckon,' says Mrs. Endycott. 'Nothing else that I can zee for it, cus if the ole baiste waun' go up yer he waun' climb up the 'eel us have jis come down, fer certin.'

'Can't you vind out what's the matter with the toad?' says my Ann.

All very well to tell about me vinding out what was the matter with 'n. I knawed so-much about his inzide as a cat knaws about his gran'mother. However, I remembered all-to-once that when us had similer caper once bevore, the Young Jan tooked out one o' they sparkling plugs and vound a bit o' durt on 'en, and when he clained that off 'twas all right. So I thought I mid-so-well chance it. 'Twould look as if I was doing zummat, even if it did'n do no gude.

So I lifted up the lid and had a wrench and unscrewed a sparkling plug. Fus' one I come to. The women-volk was stood around gap-mouthid to zee me do sitch thing.

And I be dalled if there wad'n a bit o' muck lied right across they li'l pin-points. 'Twad'n much bigger'n a gnat's eye, but I knawed he'd no business there. So I clained 'n off and putt back the sparkling plug again, near as possible as I vound 'n,

59

wondering all the time whether I was doing right or no.

'Jump in,' I says. But not they wude'n.

'You draive on a bit, and us'll walk to the top o' the 'eel,' they said.

So I wind up the ingine, and got up in me sate. And bother me if I had'n done the right thing. Ole Biskit went away like a two-year-old. Up over the nap jis' like one train.

'Wo, stop,' they 'olleyed. 'Us'll get up now.'

But I was veeling wicked.

'I durzen stop,' I says. 'I'll wait fer 'ee up head o' the 'eel.'

And by jo, 'twas a doost of a way to the top. I keeped on turning around cornders, and there was still more 'eel gwain up. When I did stop, to-last, I had to wait fer quarter-nower before they dragged up tired as dugs.

'Twad'n right thing to do, I'll admit, but it larned they a lesson. They was a lot more polite to me arter that. But 'twas a gude job 'twas nothing else but the sparkling plug, cus that was the only thing I knowed.

Us did'n have no more trouble arter that genst us got to Lynton and putt the Ole Biskit into the garridge. And I tell 'ee straight I was glad nuff to zee the back aw'n fer a bit.

But us had bin longer time on the rawd that I ordained fer to be, and 'twas weighing heavy on me mind about the journey back along. I couldn' get they tremenjis 'eels out o' me haid, and what would hap'm if aught was to go wrong half-ways down. Two or dree times the women-folk passed remark to me and I never tooked a bit o'nawtice, 'cus I was picshering the whole lot gwain haidlong down over a precipice a hunderd mile a minute and nothing to zave us from distruction.

'What's the matter with 'ee, cheel?' says my Ann. 'You'm walking about like a man-a-lost. Be 'ee slape and draiming, or deeve, or what?'

'I know what 'tis,' says Mrs. Snell. 'The poor feller wants a drink. He ab'm had a drop o' nort zince us left 'ome. Do 'ee go and get yerzel' zummat, Jan.'

'I thought us was all gwain in zomeplace and have tay,' I says.

'What do you want with ole tay-watter?' her says. 'You wants zummat differnt to that ole slatter. That's the wist of having a paasel of ole women-volk hanged on to 'ee. Daun' 'ee wish you'd got a man along with 'ee fer comp'ny?'

60

I could a-said I would like the Young Jan to draive back the car. But I did'n want to make 'em any more narvous than what they was.

'That's all right, Mrs. Snell,' I says. 'If I wants aught I'll go an' get it.'

'So do 'ee,' her says.

However. Us went in one o' they caffey plaaces and had a bit o' zummat. And very nice 'twas too, and I veeled all the better for it till they tole me how much 'twas to pay, and then I'm jiggered if I wad'n properly frightened.

I was itching to start back 'ome cus I was feared o' the dark coming on. But they women-volk wanted to look about the plaace a bit fust. Us went to zee thik funny li'l ole train arrangement what slides down the side o' the 'eel to Lynmouth. I was fer riding down and up again, jis to say us had been. But us couldn' get Mrs. Endycott in the mind aw't.

'I wouldn' go down there,' her said, 'not fer a stocking full o' suvrins. Spausin' the ole thing was to break, where should us be to then?'

'You'd get down there all the zame,' I says.

'Ees,' her says, 'and I'd like to come back all he zame if you daun' mind. Not be clained off the wall with a bucket o' watter and a brish.'

Us tried to persuade her 'twas safe as houzes, but 'twad'n no gude.

Wull, so then us trapesed around and viewed a vew more things. But I was on wires all the time wanting to be off, cus I couldn' help thinking about they ole 'eels, and what would hap'm if Ole Biskit tooked it into his head to be contr'y.

But do you think I could get 'em to make-'ase? Not I couldn'.

I keep on throwing out hints like. 'Us better be getting away now, purty quick,' I'd say; 'otherways 'twill come in dark avore us gets 'ome.'

And best aw't was, they'd agree with me every time.

'Thass right,' they'd say, 'us muzzen draive it along too laate.'

Then us would pokee along fer a yard or two, and I'd think us was doing butiful, when all-to-once one aw'm would make a rish for a shop winder like a bull at a gaate.

'There, lookee, there's a hat zac'ly like the one Mrs. Coombes had on to church las' Zindy. Zac'ly the feller to 'en, only hers was

61

a differnt colour and a bit more bowed behind and more flat
'pon-tap. You never sees a hat like that to the shops to
Barleycombe.'

Then they'd bide there yapping about every other hat in the
winder, till I'd zay, 'Do you knaw 'tis getting laate, and if aught
should hap'm on the rawd us'll be in a purty vine pickle.'

Then they'd all zay, 'Ees, come on. 'Tis time us was starting.'

So us got on a bit o' ways, and then 'twould be:

'How should 'ee like a pair o' they cannle-sticks, Mrs. Stewer?
My Aunt Susie had the identical feller pair to they, only hers was
a wider shape at the bottom and round instaid o' square, and
hers was only dree cannles and they takes vive. Otherwise you
wouldn' know 'em apart.'

'If I had my choice I'd have one o' they fruit dishes. They looks
butiful with a couple o' bananas in 'em.'

Aw, my dear 'art alive!

'What you'd better have,' I says, 'is a veather bed so's you can
make yerzel's comferable bezide the rawd if us gets hanged up in
the dark.'

I was beginning to get a bit narked, I can tell 'ee, cus I could
zee all manner o' things cropping up. Sparkling plugs what
wouldn' sparkle, and wheels getting pumshers and the ole car
rinning away down the 'eels and all the rest aw't. But I'm blawed
if I cude'n a-drove dree calves to market quicker than what I cude
get they dree women droo thikky strate. And the begger aw't
was, they'd keep on repaiting 'Us mus' be getting along. 'Tis time
us was on the rawd.'

'Yes, us mus' be getting along. There, lookee-zee, Mrs. Snell,
there's the very thing I bin looking fer this years; a tay-pot with a
sainsible top to 'en. I do abominate they tay-pots where the lid be
orwis valling off into the cup.'

And mind you, her'd bin looking fer't fer years, but her did'n
go an' purchase it. No. All her wanted was to stand there and
gake at 'n. And t'others assisted her, like dree bullicks looking at
nothing and wondering what would come of it.

'Be you ever coming or no?' I says to-last.

'Bless the man, whatever's got 'ee?' says Ann. 'Us be coming
zo-vast as us can. Do 'ee expect us to run?'

However. I got 'em there evenchally and putt Ole Biskit all
raddy to start.

62

'Arf-minute,' I says. 'I mus' jis get a bit o' baccy. I ab'm got nuff to last me home.'

Caw! I'm jiggered! Mind you, there was a baccyshop right across the strate. I'll make a bet you couldn' count a score bevore I was gone and back again, but I'm blawed if my missis did'n kick up bobs-a-dy.

'What a man 'tis,' her saith. 'Yer you bin poking about all the arternune, and now when everybody be anxious to start you'm wasting time rinning about all over the plaace. 'Twill be dark as a bag avore us gets 'ome.'

And I'm popped if 'twad'n, too. Lucky Ole Biskit was in gude timper and went along butiful. But us tooked the wrong turning twice and went miles out the way. And 'tis tayjis job draiving with they ole lamps when you ban't accustomed to it. One plaace I stapped and axed a chap how much vurder 'twas to Barnstable.

'You ban't on the Barnstable rawd,' he says. 'You'm gwain to Ilfracombe.'

Dear, dear, dear! Us had to meander droo all manner o' li'l ole by-lanes avore us got back in turnpike again. And mother said, 'I knawed us was on the wrong rawd.'

'Then why fer gudeness saake had'n 'ee said zo before?' I says.

'What's gude o' me saying aught?' her says. 'You will have yer awn way, but I knawed us was wrong.'

And zo, to-last, us arrived back to Muddlecombe in the daid waste and middle o' the night, howers later than us ordained, and me properly worn out and tired as a dog.

But I thought it putt the capper on it when mother said:

'Well, 'tis yer awn fau't. You should have started back sooner.'

'Caw! I says, 'if that id'n zummat! Arter me keeping on to 'ee all the arternune and couldn' get 'ee to move.'

'However can 'ee say such thing?' her says, 'when us was sot up there in the ole car all raddy and waiting to start, and you rinning about all over the plaace buying baccy.'

Darn my rigs! What can 'ee do with 'em?

CHAPTER ELEVEN

A day of surprises, from the last of which Jan learns a lesson.

You muzzen think that every time I goes out with Ole Biskit I
haves accident. I shouldn' like fer you to think that, cus it wouldn'
be true. Matter o' fac', I've got like that now, so's I can draive
purty much where I mind to, and laive word bevore I starts what
time I be gwain to get home.

'Twad'n orwis like it. One time I used to fix the time to start and
laive it to Ole Biskit to say when us would return; or whether us
ever returned at all or no. But now I thinks nothing o' starting off
fer Exeter or Barnstable or Plymouth. I must a-bin hunderds o
'miles, one time and t'other.

Still, I gets a shock zometimes, even now. T'other day I had
sivverl shocks, right off the reel.

Me and mother and my darter Jane and the Young Jan was all
gwain to ride into Exeter fer the day. Us left home quarter arter
ten by the clock in the kitchen and he'm half-a-nower an' twenty
minutes too vast. Us keeps 'n like that fer ketching trains.

I got me fus' shock right to the very start. When I went out to
get in the car the others was there bevore me; and when I zeed
that the Young Jan was sot up in the back sate along o' mother I
took it fer granted that he meant fer me to draive.

Jane was sot up in the draiver's sate, fiddling about with the
guiding wheel, pretending her was making the car to go, like the
chillern will do zometimes. So I made meanings to her to make
rume fer me.

'Let me draive, shall I?' her says.

'Ees,' I says, 'you'd draive zummat fer certin. Draive anybody
mazed is about the extaint o' your draiving, I reckon.'

'I daun' zee why I shouldn' draive,' her says. 'Only turn this-yer
wheel about, and kick they li'l things with yer veet zometimes.
That's all you do's. I could do that.'

64

'Daun' be zilly,' I says. 'There's sight more to it then you thinks. Shift along an' let me come there. Us waun' reach Exeter to-day else.'

Young Jan had dapped around to the front, in raddiness to turn the starting hannle.

'Let Jane try a li'l ways, uncle,' he says. 'Her'll zoon vind her mistaake.'

'Rummage,' I says. 'Her'll tear the thing abroad and then us wude be in a purty vine pickle.'

'Well, anyhow,' says the maid, 'let me hold the wheel a bit arter the ingine's started. 'Twill veel more like real when he's making proper noise.'

'What a baaby thee art, all-to-once,' I says. 'I'd be 'shamed aw't, a grawed-up young wumman.'

Her laafed like anything, and Young Jan started the ingine gwain. I wad'n troubling mezel' very much, cus o' cou'se the car wad'n in gear so he cude'n travel.

'Daun' you go titching they hannles,' I says, 'else there'll be accident.'

Laur massey! The words wad'n hardly out o me mouthe when her went messing about with the gear hannle and bevore I could stop the blessid thing us started to move. And with the zame, Young Jan drapped up over the zide o' the car and into the back sate wai'out stapping to open the door.

My dear zaul! I was frightened out o' me life. Us travelled out o' the garridge into the coort and I couldn' zee nothing for it but rinning slap into the wall o' the houze.

'Stop 'n quick,' I holleyed. 'Putt on the brake.'

But instead o' putting on the brake her pulled the wrong hannle and putt the ole thing in second gear. Natterally, instead o' stapping us went vaster. And there was I jumping about and holleying to the maid what to do, and her did'n do none of it.

And us did'n rin slap into the wall o' the houze, neether. Her pulled the guiding wheel around and us started out droo the coort.

'Daun' 'ee try to draive droo the gate, stoobid,' I says. And believe me or believe me not, if her did'n put one hand on my arm.

'Sit still, dad,' her says. 'I can't draive proper if you keeps jumping about so.'

65

By this time us was close to the gate. I knowed what that gate meant. There wad'n more'n zix inches to spare eether zide. How many times had I 'itched up all vower wheels, one to a time, trying to get past. And the rate Jane was making for it I cude zee nothing but tearing off a wheel or knacking over a paust.

And bevore I could make up me mind which 'twas gwain to be, us turned out on the rawd and went licking along like winky. I tell 'ee I zot back like a man in a draime.

And 'twad'n as if us was wommling about, or rinning in the ditch, or aught like o' that. Us was coosing along straight as a line, and Jane looking out over the tap o' the wheel as suant as a basket o' chips.

'Mind this-yer cornder,' I holleyed when us come to Jan Grant's. Tis a nasty bend in the rawd jis there. Orwis makes me narvous gwain around thik cornder. 'Take care,' I says, 'you'm gwain too vast.'

And that there darn maid (ever I shude say such thing) her turned her face around to me, when her should a-bin looking where her was draiving to, and her smiled to me. Her ought to a-bin frightened out of her zeb'm sainses, by gude rights, and I tell 'ee, her smiled. And time her'd finished smiling us was around the bend and licking along the straight. Her hadn't took no more account than if her was draiving a dunkey.

Cou'se, up to now I had'n had what you might call time to think. I was so tooked a-back, my haid was gwain around like a wirly-gig. But when my idayas beginned to zettle down again I thought it strange the way they two was behaving behind. 'Twas vunny they should be zo quiet. You'd a-thought mother wude a-bin up in arms, and raddy to jump out over the zide. But when I turned around, there her was lied back as comferable as you plaise, looking as if her had'n got a care in the world.

I spause there must a-bin zummat amusing about the look on my faace, cus they both bust out laafing. I got a bit narked, I can tell 'ee. 'I'm glad you can zee the joke,' I says. 'I spause I ban't hardly so sharp as some people.'

'Daun' be so stoobid,' says Ann. 'Tell the maid her's doing very well, and not imagine you'm the only one with sufficient sainse to draive a car.'

'Id'n doing so bad, is she, uncle, fer a fust attemp'?' says the Young Jan.

'I'll "fust attemp"' you,' I says, and then all the lot of 'em laafed like billy-o.

'Look yer, young wumman,' I says to Jane, 'how many times have you two young volks had out this car without my knowledge?'

'Aw,' says Jane, screwing up her faace as if her was trying to think, 'what would it be? About of–twice, would it be, Jan?'

'I should think,' says the young rascal, 'in and out, taking one time with another, 'twould be about of twice.'

'Twice what?' I says.

'Twice six.' And then they all bust out laafing again, and I thought the bes' thing fer me was to join in along with 'em. You mid depend, 'tis wisest thing when you've bin had. 'Tis quickest way out. And the maid said, 'You ban't vexed with me, dad, be 'ee?'

'Giddout with 'ee, vexed,' I says. 'You'm doing cabbical.'

And I'm jiggered if her wad'n, too. Caw, bless me, her took it so aisy as if it wad'n no more than turning a zewing machine.

And did'n I say that that there blimming Ole Biskit knawed? Of cou'se he knaws. When fust I tried to draive 'n he sot up all the capers imaginable. Speshly if there was anybody about and I wanted to show off a bit. He'd spit and cough and jib and play 'amlet. But now, with the maid behind 'en, bless yer 'art he went along so-proud as a paycock, and never looked right ner left. Properly sticked his head up in the air he did, like the fus' prize winner in a trotting match. Us flipped into Exeter in no time.

While us was into the city the rain come on turrable. It stopped again bevore us started home but the rawds was hawful mucky, so I said to Jane, 'I think I'd better-way draive back along, cus 'twill be heavy gwain.' But her beggid of me to let her draive. 'I should mortle like to zay I drove all the way in and back again,' her said. And mother said, 'Let the maid finish the job if her want to, now her've started.'

Plaise yerzel',' I says, 'but I reckon 'tis a bit too much fer her. Daun' blame me if us gets chucked out.'

'Gude laur!' says Ann, 'I've never blamed 'ee fer the stoobid things you've done yerzel', so I'm sure I shan't blame 'ee fer other folks's mistaakes.'

However. Jane took the reins, or the wheel I should say, and us started off. Everything went all right till us got to Tottles's

Cross, and then her turned left-handed to go in around Barleycombe, cus Young Jan said 'twas the better rawd. Better than
gwain through Week village.

Well, o' cou'se, gwain that way you passes by the clay-pits,
there to Storget. I'd never drove around that way mezel', but fer a
mile or zo the rawd was inches deep with clay, off the wheels o'
the carts. And I spause the rain falling on it, and so much travvic,
'twas all graisy, jis' like butter.

I was sot back behind along o' mother this time, and the Young
Jan was in front with Jane. And all-to-once us had a vunny
roundy-go sort o' sinsation, jis like's if the world had suddenly
jumped back the wrong way. The hedges went flipping across the
rawd, and the trees an' the tall chumleys was dancing the Rigs o'
Lunnon. Mother gived a shout, and Young Jan holleyed zummat
to Jane, and arter a bit it all went quiet again and everything got
still. And when us come to look, there was Ole Biskit turned right
around the wrong way with two wheels in the ditch.

'Whatever have hap'm'd?' I says.

''Tis nort,' says the boye. 'Only a bit of a skid.'

'What do 'ee mean, nort?' I says. 'You call that nort? I call it a
doost of a lot. Why, us might as well all bin killed. Whatever was
'ee thinking of, maid?'

''Twad'n Jane's fau't,' says Young Jan, spaiking up purty sharp.
'The best draiver in the world can't avoid that. Ole Biskit slipped
on this-yer graisy ole clay, and if Jane had'n kep' calm and done
what I said 'twould a-bin a sight wiss.'

'Rummage,' I says. 'When he started capering about her ought
to have kep' tight hold to the wheel and made'n go straight, not
let'n turn around that fashin. I ban't blaming you, my dear,' I says,
'but it wanted zomebody with more experience, and stronger in
the arm to master 'en, and not let'n have his haid. I'd better take
'en on, same's I said when us started.'

Mind you, I wad'n altogether sorry, cus I thought 'twould larn
'em a lesson not to trait me with sitch scorn another time. Young
Jan wanted to argue the point, but Jane wouldn' let'n to. Her was
turrable white-facid, poor maid, and her wad'n lofe to let me take
her plaace.

'Well, you take care, uncle,' says the boye, and not too sweet
by half. 'You've no idaya what 'tis like when you gets a proper
skid.'

68

He was only saying that to shield the maid. Or that's what I considered.

However. I got the car around straight, and started off. 'Go stiddy, uncle,' says the boye. He was sot up bezide me now, and Jane in the back seat with her mother. He erritated me with his 'Go stiddy,' and his 'Take care,' like's if I wad'n capable, as well as he. So I dersay I travelled a bit more rapid than what I should else. I had to go around a bit of a cornder. Nothing very much; only a bend in the rawd.

But nobody ever bended like it, bevore ner since.

What hapm'd, zac'ly, I can't tell 'ee, cus I shall never knaw. But all of a sudden I veeled as if the ole car had bin pulled away from me and jerked to one zide. 'Twas sitch a quare sinsation that I come all over to a creem, and I turned the wheel quick to make'n come back again. But he wouldn' come back. He went on turning the oppozyte way to what I was guiding. Then wai'out the laistest warning he started to go zideways, bang fer the hedge. And just as he was gwain in the ditch he changed his mind and flipped off to the other side o' the rawd. Arter that I dunnaw what he done. He was sliding about like a lump of ice on a sheet o' glass. I had'n no more control over'n than I had over the mune. He shot vifty ways at once. Everybody was jumping up and holleying, and Young Jan baaled zummat in my yer-awl, but I couldn' sainse it, cus me wits was skitting about like a bit o' paaper in a gale o' wind. 'Twas jis' like's if you'd putt a vat ole dumman on a pair o' skates fer the fus' time in her life and give her a gude hard shove. I never veeled so helpless in me life. Ole Biskit sim to be doing ten things to-once. Then he'd waltz a bit. Then he'd hop-skip-an'-jump. Then one side the rawd, then the t'other. Then vore a bit, then back a bit. Sliding, slipping, turning, twesting.

And then, all-to-once, he flinged hiszel' right around, hind part bevore, and away-da-go back in the derection us had come. With the zame, another turrable slip zideways, two wheels up in the bank, and 'out you goes, neck an' crop.' Up in the air goes Ole Biskit, and come to a stan'still, two wheels on the rawd and two pointing up to the sky.

Us was all shot out, tap-an-tail into the mud. And there us lied fer a minute or two, till us come to our sainses. Fust I looked to zee if I was killed. Then I looked to zee how many bones was broke. And when I found there wad'n no bones broke I looked around to zee how many o' the rest was dead. But they was all rubbing theirsel's, in differnt plaaces, according to the manner in which they'd landed on the ground.

'Twas a lucky thing Ole Biskit vinished up on his side, and did'n turn clane over. If he had a-done us would all a-bin killed fer certin. The rawd was littered up with everything that wad'n screwed in; cushions, tin cans, tools, all mother's arrants, even the boards us rest our veet on. You never zeed sitch a mess in all your born days. And us all plastered with muck from haid to voot.

Mother was the fust to vind her tongue.

'What you wants at these times,' her saith, 'is zomebody experienced and strong in the arm, and daun' blame me if you gets chucked out. All you got to do is to keep tight hold to the wheel and make'n go straight. You mus' let'n zee that you'm master over'en, and not let'n turn around. Jane, I'ope you've took notice o' the way yer vather do's it, so's you'll know how to manage nex' time, and not stop halfways through, like you did bevore. You did'n do it proper. You mus' go to the dancing class and pick up a vew more steps. You did'n complete the figger.'

Sarve me right. Sarve me jolly gude right. I did'n ought to have said I was master over Ole Biskit. He yeard me say it, and he knaws. Nobody waun' make me believe but what Ole Biskit knaws.

CHAPTER TWELVE

An exciting drive in which Jan quite expects to be blown up.

Barleycombe Turmut Vair is orwis the fust Wainsdy in November. 'Tis a big day into Barleycombe, Turmut Vair be, and you'll vind purt' near everything in the world in Barleycombe on that day, barrin' turmuts. Same as Ingyen Vair to Newton Abbot where you can zee any mortle thing seps ingyens, and Goozey Vair to Tavistock where you can vind 'most everything but the geeze.

I went in to Turmut Vair in Ole Biskit, and vinished my business and I was draiving back home along, in the early part o' the arternune. I was all alone, and jis' as I passed the Oss an' Jockey I zeed a li'l boye walking on ahaid in the rawd. I reckoned I owned him for a Muddlecombe cheel, so I pulled up bezide 'n.

'Ban't you Mrs. Weskit's li'l boye?' I says.

'Yezzur, I be, zur,' he said. Had to look right up, he did, cus he wad'n much higher than the top o' the wheel. And properly loaded up with passels he was, too, poor li'l chap.

'I thought you was,' I says. 'Where be you gwain?'

'Plaise zur, home, zur.'

'What, and carr' all they arrants! Id'n nobody coming agenst 'ee?'

'Plaise zur, no, zur.'

'Aw, dear me,' I says. 'You'll be tired to death carr'ing that lot vower mile. Would you like to jump up and ride along o' me?'

'Yezzur. I would, zur, plaise, zur.'

'I'd got a heap o' things up bezide o' me, so I putt the li'l chap in the sate behind. And the innocent li'l faace aw'n looking so plaised to think he did'n have to trapes all that long distance.

'Your mother have brought you up to very nice behaviour,' I says. And he said, 'Yes, zur, plaise, zur.'

So I draived on again. But I'm blawed, in that li'l journey, if I did'n have a peck o' trouble. I veeled more sorry fer the li'l tacker than what I did fer mezel', cus 'twas nuff to frighten the life out of

71

anybody. And he never in a moter-car bevore in his life.

Us had'n gone more'n hunderd yards bevore there was sitch a tremenjis 'BANG!' Purt' near made me jump droo me hat.

I thought to mezel' at once, 'That's a tyre bust, fer certin.'

I never had'n had sitch thing hap'm to Ole Biskit bevore, but I yeard one go off once into Barleycombe Raaces, and 'twas like a gun, zac'ly. And this was jis' the zame, so I guessed what 'twas in a minute. I was turrable vexed about it, cus I wad'n properly sure whether I knowed the way to putt on the odd wheel or no.

However, I draived into the zide and stapped as quick as I could.

'You need'n be frightened,' I says to the li'l feller. ''Tis only the weel gone pop.'

'Yes, zur. Is that what 'tis, zur?' he says.

Very nice manners, he'd a-got, sure nuff. But I knawed that Mrs. Weskit was orwis very pa'ticler in larning her chillern the way to spaik proper.

So I got out to zee which weel 'twas busted. But they was all right. Blawed up tight, same's when I started.

'That's quare,' I says to the cheel.

'Yezzur, 'tis, zur.'

'You yeard 'n go pop, did'n 'ee?'

'Yezzur. I thought praps you was shatting to a rabbut zur.'

'Nonsainse, rabbut,' I says. 'But I dersay 'twas somebody shatting t'other zide the hedge, now you come to mention it.'

'Yezzur, very likely 'twas, zur.'

Be-as-'twill, I started again. But us had'n gone no distance hardly, when, 'BANG!' goes again. I hap'm to be turning a cornder at the time, and it give me sitch a start, 'twas all the wonders in the world I had'n drove right in the ditch. When I stapped, Ole Biskit was a-thurt the rawd, and if there'd bin anything coming us must have collised fer certin.

Poor li'l tacker was looking out over the zide.

'Is it the weel this time, zur?' he says.

'No, 'tid'n a weel,' I says. 'But you need'n be feared. 'Tid'n nothing that's gwain to hurt 'ee.'

'No, zur. Thank'ee, zur,' he said.

But although I said so, jis to pacify the cheel, I did'n know hardly whether 'twas or no. I couldn' think where to look fer the cause aw't, nuther. However, I titched a thing or two, yer and

there, to comfert the li'l feller, and then I said, 'There, he waun'
do it again, now.'

'No, zur,' he said, and I derzay he thought I was a wonderful
chap to putt'n to rights so aisy.

'You'm a brave li'l man,' I says, 'not to be frightened,' and he
said he was.

Well, then us went on all right fer a bit, but all-to-once, 'BANG!
BANG!! BANG!!! BANG!!!!' Vower of 'em.

'My dear zaul,' I says, 'his very bowels in gwain to blow out.'

I jumped out, quick's possible, and I'm beggered if I wad'n
proper gallied this time. I expected to zee the whole contraption
vly right up in the air.

Wull, and then I remembered the Young Jan telling something
about a 'back-vire.' I did'n pay very much 'tention to it at the
time, but I wished I had now. I knaw 'twas zummat to do with the
gas getting into the exhausted-box. I opened the lid and kaineed
in around the works, but I wouldn' knaw the exhausted-box
when I zeed it. However, I hap'm to put me hand up agin the
works and took'n away again quick, and said zummat which I
did'n ought to, in front o' the cheel.

'I zee what's the matter,' I says, 'he've got too 'ot. Us'll have to
let'n sit a bit, and coldee.'

So I let'n bide fer vive or tain minutes with the lid off, and kep'
spaiking to the boye to keep his sperrits up. I was feared he'd
want to jump out and walkee, and tell 'ee the truth, I did'n want
to be left alone.

Then us started again, and fer a bit us went along butiful, when
all of a sudden, 'BANG!' Laur-a-massey, I thought the whole
consarn was gwain to the vower winds of heab'm.

But by thees time I'd got properly desprit. There wad'n but a
mile left to go and I thought to mezel', 'If you want to bust, you
bust.'

So instaid o' stapping thees time I putt me voot on the ole
acsillyrater and made'n go as vast as possible.

Caw! My dear days. You never yerd sitch a racket in all your
life. The vaster us did go the more he did bang. 'Twas like the
start of another war. Us might a-bin one o' they ole tanks gwain
across the battle-vield. Volks come rishing out o' their houses to
zee what could be gwain past. Women ketched up their baabies
and carried 'em inzide the gaates. The dogs come rinning out to

vind out what the row was about, and join in as best they could. But laur bless 'ee, no dog had'n got a chance to make hiszel' heard in that racket.

I was expecting every minute that there 'd be one bang bigger than all the rest and I'd go up and never come down again, and us slewed around Jan Grant's cornder on two weels and through Muddlecombe strate like a vire-ingine.

I ought to a-stapped to the Chapel by gude rights and let the boye get out. But I was feared to stap, case I'd never start again. I could zee me awn doors, and I was determined to get there or die in the attemp'.

The poor li'l tacker was holleying to me from behind to stop. But if it had bin the king holleying I wude'n a-stopped. 'Twas jist a question now whether I'd ride to me awn gaate or be blowed there.

And when I did stop, to-last, if thik poor li'l feller wad'n out over the zide bevore the w'eels had done gwain around, and off home like a dog tail-piped.

And I wad'n very fur behind 'n, I can assure 'ee.

The racket us was making fetched out mother and the maid, and the Young Jan. I can tell 'ee this much, and 'tis the truth if I never move again, I was never so glad to zee thik young feller in all me life.

'What's matter, uncle?' he says.

''Tis thikky-there darned ole exhausted-box,' I says. I was anxious he should knaw that I understood what was the matter with 'n.

'Well, he'm exhausted now all right,' he says. 'He'm so-quiet as a lamb.'

'He'm all right when he'm stood still,' I says. ''Tis drec'ly you begins to move. You draive'n a bit and zee.'

Young Jan putt his voot on the stap to nip up in the sate, when, 'BANG!!!' he goes right under our very noses. And with the zame, up goes a strame o' vire and smock, right in the middle o' the car.

My hyvers! Young Jan never titched the ground till he was inzide the gate, and that's ten veet, every inch aw't. Ner I did'n neether.

'Look out,' he 'olleys. 'Stan' back, everybody. The petrol tank's avire. He'll explode in a minute.'

The women-volk disappeared in-houze, and me and the boye stood back out the way. Ole Biskit was blazing away and powering out sparks and smeech nuff to chuck 'ee.

'What can us do!' I says.

'Us can't do nothing till the petrol's gone,' he says. 'It might all blaw up now any minute. What fer gudeness saake is aunt doing? Go back, aunt!'

Mother was rishing out droo the coort gaate with a bucket o' watter.

'That waun' do no gude,' he holleyed 'Keep back, aunt, 'twill do more hurt than gude,'

But he was too laate. Her emp' the bucket o' water right in the car.

"Twill make the vire rin about all over the plaace,' says the Young Jan. But it did'n. It made it out.

'Fetch out a clath, Jane,' says mother, 'and wipe'n out.'

Purty gude mess he was in with the bucket o' watter slattered all over the vloor. However, they got it clained out all right.

And then all-to-once mother started to laaf.

"Tis nothing to laaf about,' I says. 'I might a-bin burned to death.'

'Ees,' her says, 'and if you'd bin Ole Guy Vox you wude a-bin burned fer certin.'

'What do 'ee mean?' I says. But while I said the words a 'orrible thought come in me mind. I remembered that Barleycombe Turmut Vair was orwis fus' Wainsdy in November.

And with the zame mother held up a han'ful o' they ole vireworks, all black and busted, where they'd bin let off.

'I'm popped if li'l Jimmy Weskit ab'm had you on proper,' her says. 'He've bin letting off they vireworks all the way 'ome, and he must-left a gurt toad burning when he jumped out.'

'Twas only too true. And now us be the laafiing-stock o' the parrish.

When I ketch hold to thik younger rinagate I'll give he Vith o' November, I will. And me telling of'n he'd got sitch nice manners, too.

EXIT OLE BISKIT

In course of time Jan Stewer became a more or less expert driver, and in his ancient car visited many parts of the West Country. But in proportion as his skill increased, so his journeys, while being taken in greater comfort to himself, ceased to provide incidents for narratives. Jan's early inexperience, however, left its mark on the car, which, at the end of its career was not, to say the least, a thing of beauty. Biskit's days of usefulness are now over and we leave the old car with the following farewell verses, written by Jan after his final journey:-

You ban't exac'ly hanzum and you ban't exac'ly new;
In fact, you'm old and hugly if I mus' say what is true.
Your bonnet don't shut vitty and your hood is frightful torn;
Your paint and varnish I might say is pra'tically gorn.

You'm nothing of a ornament, a body must admit.
Your wings won't make a angel of 'ee by a gudish bit.
I mind when they curved nicely round, and butiful they shone;
They looks now like a ole top-hat what have been sot upon.

I mind your lamps when they was smart, but now they gives me pain.
They'm looking like ole tin cans what have been out in the rain.
Your seats is gone in plaaces and the stuffing's showing through;
I has to use a bit o' string to keep the doors shut to.

And I wude'n call 'ee quiet, not compared with zome volks' toys,
To tell the honest truth you makes a diggens of a noise.
You've got a nasty habit, too, of spitting, which is rude;
And you'd think, to hear the racket, your inside was come unscrewed.

The journeys us have had of late have all been took on trust.
'Twas question whe'er you'd go or stop, or fall abroad, or bust.

OLE BISKIT

Still, you kep' on pegging zome'ow, or you had a darn gude
    try—
But now I'm feared the time have come when us must say,
    'Gude-bye.'

Yet all the zame, Ole Biskit, you've a-bin a real gude friend,
And no one shan't abuse 'ee now you'm nearly out to-end.
Though you'd got old and shaky, yet you always done your best;
You sarved me well, Ole Biskit, and you've arned your bit o' rest.

And zometimes when I looks at 'ee there comes into my mind
A thought which shows that I be getting childishly inclined;
It zeems to me as if—of course I knows it can't be true—
As if you thinks the same of me as what I thinks of you.

OTHER TALES

IMPROVING THE MIND

How a Literary and Debating Society was formed at Muddlecome.

Purty fine capers up to our Insichute, I'm jiggered!

The committee have invented a new gyte, which they reckons will improve the minds of the common volks, and larn 'em to be upsides with the paasens and the turneys and sitch-like, in the matter of standing up and holding forth in public, like a Mimber o' Parlyment, or the chap in the market what cures corns.

'Tis amazing what a host o' people there is gwain about anxious to improve other volks' minds. They can't zee a body with a hungry-looking faace and a ragged ole suit o' cloas without they'm busting to improve his mind.

I dersay 'tis all right, and he'd be all the better for it, no doubt, but I zeem 'twould be more vitty-like if they was to improve his stommick a bit fust. I suppose 'tid'n so much expainse improving anybody's mind as what 'tis to improve his stommick, and that's why there's so many willing to undertake it.

'Tis amazing what a quantity of advice you can give away without costing 'ee a varden.

Mind, I ban't rinning out agin advice. 'Tis a very gude thing provided you daun' get too much aw't. Only, advice is zummat like docter's medicine; 'tid'n a bit o'gude unless you takes it. Reading the label on the bottle waun' do.

And I ban't saying a word agin improving the mind. I dersay us cude all do with a bit aw't. Only you wants to be careful what soort o'mind it is to start with. I remember once, a young chap was put to work as a clurk in a plaace o'business, and he had'n bin there very long bevore he started writing other volks' names on the cheques and putting the money into his awn pocket. But he wad'n very

81

clever at it and they very zoon found 'n out, and he was carr'd up bevore the jidge.

However, the jidge was very laynient with 'n, and seeing he was sitch a young feller and never done nothing o' the soort bevore, he wouldn' sen' 'en to prisin this time. He ordered 'n to be putt away to a plaace where they would improve his mind. And I'm blawed if they did'n improve his mind to sitch extent, that they nex' place he went to he was able to chait so well that they did'n ketch 'en at it for years.

You daun' want to go putting dressing on dashels.

However, that id'n neether yer ner there. This yer 'improvement' caper was started fer a very gude purpose, and I 'ope 'twill succeed, although the fus' beginning wad'n hardly what anybody would call promising. Still, of cou'se, you can't expect to have everything all-to-once. Or if you do you won't get it.

'Tis what they caals a 'Littery and Debating Society.' That's the naame it go'th by. What it do mean, zac'ly, I can't tell'ee. But they've got one o' the sort into Barleycombe, and they tell'th me they haves 'em to Exeter and Plymouth. And even up to Lunnon, so I've been given to understand, but I can't answer for that.

Be that as it may, us never likes fer Muddlecombe to be behind other plaaces, although us be only a smaal parrish in a manner o' spaiking. And so 'twas mooted for us to have one o' these things of our own.

'Cou'se, a few o' the bettermos' volk was the ins'igation aw't. Squire and his laady, and paasen and his wive, and Doctor Jinkins and his missis and one or two bezides, they hatched up this-yer caper between 'em. They'm, like, the committee o' the Insichute, zee, and they'm orwis scheming fer fresh idayas to intice the volks to attaind. So they give nawtice that there was gwain to be a meetin' to discuss the matter o' this-yer new society, and there was scores attainded, 'cus twad'n like's if you had to pay to go in. You can orwis depaind on having a-plenty there if 'tis free-gracious. But if 'tis zummat to pay 'tis wonderful what excuses they will hatch up.

However. Us had the parrish well represented, as they do say on the paapers. Docter Jinkins he was the cheerman, up higher end o' the rume, and squire and paasen and the rest o' the committee lot, they was sot both sides aw'n, to paust 'n up in the matter o' this-yer mind-improving. They was facing towards we, like they would if they was gwain to give intertainment.

Wull then, in the front rove 'o cheers there was a vew o' the women-volk what regards theirsel's a bit above the average, like; the wives o' the big varmers, and the skulemissis, and Tilda Grinnaway the dressmaker, and Miss Peters what lived up to Lunnon fer upperds o' ten years and made nothing o' seeing the King and Quane driving about in the park.

And then come two roves with nobody, only cheers. And arter that the varmers what belonged to the wives in the front sates. And then there was two more roves empty. Then come the maidens what did'n want to get too fur away from the chaps, and behind they was the chaps what did'n want to be too fur away from the maidens but had'n got the face to zit bezide 'em.

In the back sates of all was the rest o' the women from the village with their baabies. And they told each other they was thankful *their* minds did'n want improving like they what had the chick to poke theirsel's right up in the front.

Stood up at the back was the men what wanted to be near the door in case the meetin' shude last on till closing-time. And out in the lobby was the policeman where he could be handy to both plaaces.

And when us was all sot down what was gwain to sit down, and got middling quiet, Docter Jinkins rised up and made a spaich to bring everybody acquainted with what 'twas all about.

'The idaya,' he says, 'is to have a Littery and Debating Society all of our own, yer to Muddlecombe, like they have to other plaaces.' And then he went on with a long old rigmarole about improving the mind, and a-many things us was gwain to larn which us never knowed bevore. I ferget, zac'ly, what us was gwain to larn, but I know 'twas gwain to do us a power o' gude. And I dersay 'twill, when us gets more used to it.

What it was to do, he said, was fer all the mimbers what joined the society to meet in the Insichute one aiv'min a wik, and then zomebody what had bin choosed out bevorehand would stand up and praich up a yarn about zome pa'ticler subjic'. And arter that, it would be fer anybody in the rume that liked, to get up and say what he thought about it. The ring-laider would be 'lowed half-hower start fer his yap, and the rest would have ten minutes a-piece to putt forth their views on the matter.

When the cheerman had sot down the paasen got up and made up a long oration on the subjic.' 'Twas fus'-raate idaya, he

83

reckoned, and he 'oped that everybody would join the society and attaind the meetin's Us would be bound to larn a lot by it, he said, and 'twould improve our minds.

'Us can all larn zummat from one-t'other,' so he said, 'and never mind whether a chap's a scollard or no, he's bound to have idayas 'o zome soort which he've picked up gwain about, and 'tis orwis gude to harken to other volks' opinions. Now,' he says, 'I'd like to yer what anybody in the rume have got to say on the matter, and whether 'tis the general wish of everybody that us should have such a society or no.'

Paasen had'n hardly sot down bevore Ned Annaferd was up on his hine ligs. O' cou'se, this-yer caper was just Ned's handwriting. Anything where there's spaichifying to be done plaises he right down to the ground, speshly if he'm 'lowed to join in and putt out a vew big words.

'I think 'tis a cabbical proposial,' says Ned, 'and I shall hadvocate it to the huttermost. And I 'ope and trist,' he says, 'that one-an'-hall in this rume will support it with animosity. And not only support it, but attend to the meetin's and take part, each one according to their comprehension. Us ought to take,' he says, 'every opportunity us can to larn something fresh, and 'twould be aidyfying to one-an'-hall to be abble to come yer and harken to the peeration of anybody with knowledge in his head and the instrumentality to spit it out proper.

'And I think,' he says, ''tis a very gude idaya that arter the spaiker have vinished, others in the rume should be caaled upon to putt forth their views according to their proper consistency.'

'When you says, 'called upon,' Mr. Annafer,' says the cheerman, 'I should like for it to be understood that nobody need'n spaik unless they minds to.'

'Mr. Annaferd won't want no caaling upon, zur,' says zomebody back o' the rume. But Ned did'n take no notice of he.

'I quite railise, yer honour,' he says, 'that everybody can plaise theirsel's, and there id'n no obliteration to spaik. But with all doo rispec' to you, zur, I do 'ope that the mimbers will laive behind all modesty, and all their ole jubiousness, and spaik up according to their classification. As you have said, zur, everybody have got knowledge of zome zort in his haid, either sainsible or insainsible, and although some has'n got the jurisdiction fer putting it out same as what others have, yet 'tis marvellous what anybody can do with patience and preservation, and you mid depaind upon it, there's a-many present in this rume now, if they was to try, cude stand up and make so-gude a spaich as me or you or any other body. I shude like to zee it come to pass, and therefore I shall vote for it with the huttermost propitiation.'

Where ole Ned gets all his long words to I can't imagine. But us give'n a gude clap when he sot down, fer 'twas pretty much fer the ole feller, I reckon, to get through all that lot without doing hiszelf injury.

Well, then, Mrs. Webber axed if women was gwain to be 'lowed in, and the cheerman jumped up in a minute.

"Lowed in?' he says. 'I should think they would be 'lowed in. Us wants fer all the ladies to come, and to year what they've got to say as well as the men.'

Well, and then ole Farmer Urferd he got up and had a go at it. I could zee he'd bin itching to spaik fer zome time. Couldn' hardly contain hiszel', he couldn'.

'Paasel of ole trumpery,' he says, 'all the lot aw't, and never did'n ought to be allowed, never mind being incouraged by they what ought to knaw better. All you zeems to mind, now-a-days, is to pervide the volks with opportunity to waste their time. Purty vine pass things is coming to. 'Tis works nuff to get a job done as 'tis. What 'twill be like arter you've invented a vew more stoobid ole items I can't think. The young volks has got nuff old crams in their haids now, without you supplying 'em with any more. All they minds is rinning about to ole kickshaws. If 'tid'n vootball 'tis picshers, and if 'tid'n picshers 'tis dancing or wiss-draive, or some no-sainse ole caper like o' that. No wonder they can't get out o'bed mornings, when they'm gallivanting about half the night bevore. And now you've hatched up this redecklus scheme to larn 'em the way to talk. Talk! Bless my zaul. You daun' want no society to larn' em to do that. That's about the one an' only thing they'm capable to do, is talk. Darn'ee, they'll talk the hind leg off a dunkey. I knaw what I'm zaying, cus I've had 'em talk to me. Talk, begor. They can do that all right, without you larning aw'm.

'You daun' want no fresh capers to 'sist 'em to waste their time. Better-vit you was to putt a stap to one or two that's gwain on already. Boyes and maidens is becoming proper rinagates with so many ole kickshaws to distrac' their minds from their work. And bim-by, when they ought to be properly sot up in life, and abble to take things a bit comferable in their old age, they'll wish they had back zome o' the howers they've wasted over so much ole rummage.'

Now, if Farmer had only had the gumtion to stop there, I won't say which way the vote wude a-went, cus there was gude many of the older ones was inclined to agree wai'n. And there was sivverl more what wude'n vote one way or t'other, cus they did'n understand what 'twas all about. So I shouldn' wonder if the whole thing had'n been knock' in the haid.

But like a gude many else, he did'n knaw when he'd said nuff, so he said too much.

'And you'm trying to 'tice the women-volk in too, I zee,' he saith. 'My dear zaul, you waun' have no trouble to do that. The women will do any mortle thing sooner than bide 'ome and mind their own affairs. They'm every bit as bad as the boyes and maidens fer gadding about. The way they carries on, now-a-days is properly disgus'ful. Old women what ought to know better and set a gude example, rinning about to every doomshaw and penny-raiding that's gwain on. And who's looking arter the chillern and the house? They dunnaw, and they daun' care. And now you'm telling about perviding aw'm with zome more ole gammuts, as if they had'n got nuff already. Zend 'em 'ome too look arter their men-volk, and keep the plaace tidy. That's bes' thing fer they.

'Littery society!' he saith. 'Very gude name fer't I shude zay. There'll be a-plenty ole litter about, one sort an' another. You harken to me and putt a stap to it bevore 'tis too laate. And daun' let's year no more such ole witpot.'

Wull, and o' cou'se, by that time Farmer had sot up the back of every wumman in the plaace and they was ready to tear 'n limb from limb. And soon's the cheerman said, 'All they in favour to start the society putt up one hand,' all the women-volk sticked up one hand so-fur as they could raiche. And as there was mos'ly women in the room the mayjolity was more than the mynolity, and 'twas carried according.

OUR DEBATE

The first meeting of the Muddlecombe Literary and Debating Society. Possibly the last. Mrs. Jenkins opens with a Paper on 'Are Women the equal of Men?'

I dunnaw whether you've ever had experience of one o' thase-yer debating consarns or no. If you never ab'm, you take my tip and leave well alone. I'd sooner zee a dog-vight, mezel.'

Of course, I've yeard tell o' such things, bevore now, and I've zeed on the paapers sometimes where they've had debate in parlyment, and other plaaces, and I fancy there orwis seems to be something fishy about it. But I reckon, to zee the thing done proper you ought to have bin out yer to Muddlecombe, and witnessed the debate us had into the Insichute. 'Twould take a bit o' beating, I giv'ee my word, and 'twill be a tidy while bevore one half the popilation is on spaiking terms again with the other half.

I be glad as a burd I never had no say in the matter, cus there have been more bad-frien'ship than enough throughout the parrish, ever since thik ole debate. But luckily I kep' me mouthe shut, so they can't have nothing up agin me. And 'tis pity some o' the rest did'n do likewise. 'Twould have avoided a mortle lot of malishousness.

Of course, I blames they what started it the most. They should a-knowed better than to choose sitch a theme to arg about. They should have picked out zomething which did'n incourage people to name other volks by name. But Mrs. Jinkins with her 'aiquality of women' logic! 'Twas only edging 'em on to say things about one the other which they did'n ought to.

I knawed zac'ly what 'twas gwain to be, soon's ever I zeed what the subjic' was about. They sticked up a gurt notice outzide the Insichute and let it bide there all the wik. Up the top it said:

OUR DEBATE

MUDDLECOMBE LITTERY AND DEBATING SOCIETY
and in under:

'The fus' meeting o' the Society will be held Mondy nex', zeb'm o'clock. A Paper will be raid by *Mrs. Jinkins*, on 'Is Women the Aiqual to Men?' arter which the subjic' will be open for general discussion and Mrs. Jinkins will reply. The Mittin' will close with the usual votes o' thanks at nine o'clock.'

'I question if 'twill last that long,' I says, when I rade the notice, 'and I'll make a bet they'll be got past the thanking point in a lot less than two howers, with a subjic' like that to make remarks about.'

And they was, too.

I could zee why Mrs. Jinkins had choosed that text. 'Twas on account o' what Farmer Urferd had said about the women. Her intainded to make'n eat his words.

However. Mondy aiv'min, zeb'm o'clock, Insichute was chuck full. Farmer Urferd allowed he wad'n gwain to attaind, but he was there all right. He said he wouldn' a-went, only it had been reported that remarks was gwain to be made about 'n, and he wad'n gwain to have things said behind his back that wude'n be said bevore his faace.

Matter o' fac', Mrs. Jinkins never so much as mentioned his name, and never alluded to 'en, in no shape or form. Maister was putt out about that, I could zee he was, cus he'd made up his mind that he was gwain to be 'fronted, and when it did'n hap'm zo, he was disappointed.

Do what you will, you can never plaise some volks.

Passen was cheerman this time, and when us was all in raddiness he made up a bit of a narration, all about how the debate was to be carr'd out. Arter Mrs. Jinkins had said all her had to say, anybody was liable to get up one to a time, and spaik fer ten minutes. If they carr'd on longer than that he'd ring a bell for 'em to stop.

'I shall now ax Mrs. Jinkins to rade her paper on 'Is Women the Aiqual to Men?'' he says.

Wull, her did'n rade no paaper, more'n jist a word yer and there. All the rest her made up out of her awn haid. 'Twas mos'ly about how women did take the plaace of the men when the war was on. Zome was 'tending to the zick and wounded, and zome carr'd on the business, and zome went to work on the farms. And her'd bin told that

88

plenty o' volks should say that the women did the jobs all-so-well as the men, and better zometimes.

I'm bothered if her did'n putt it all out very well. Her's able to spaik in public as well as very many o' the men, and a darn sight better than most. How her does it all I can't think, cus her id'n but a li'l bit of a thing. I've knowed hunderds o' volks half as big again as what she is that cude'n hold a cannle to her, as regards to talking. Her can beat the paasen all to flibbits, I reckon, cus when he've got to praich a sarmon he's forced to write it all down on paaper bevorehand, and then read it off a word to a time.

Any fule cude do that. Speshly when nobody id'n allowed to get up and contrydic'. But Mrs. Jinkins her rattles it all off by rote, like the rain dropping from the orfis, without ever stopping to think.

I won't say but what if her *did* stap to think sometimes it wouldn' be all the better, cus then her wouldn' say some o' the things her do say. Or her might say 'em a bit differnt, p'r'aps.

However. Her made her spaich, and made'n very well, and most everybody clapped their hands when her sot down. Then the debate part was supposed to start.

Dr. Jinkins got up fust, and said purty much the same as his missis had said all over again, only not half so well. And then paasen he got up and said same thing over again, only not quatter so well. Then he said he should like fer zomebody in the rume to putt forth their views.

Skulemissis her went next, and her said her did'n see where the women wad'n the aiqual to the men, cus there was women docters and women lawyers, and women working on the land, and all doing so-well as what the men was.

Then Farmer Urferd got up and had a go at it. And the fun beginned. He was looking about as sweet as if he'd drinked zome of his own harvest zider by mistaake.

'What did I tell 'ee las week?' he said. 'I told 'ee this-yer caper was a paasel of ole rummage, did'n I? And now tell me if I wad'n right. Did ever anybody harken to such witpot bevore in all their life? Women the aiqual to men! Yas! In their own proper spear I'll admit. But why daun' 'em bide there? Why daun' 'em stop in their right plaace, instead o' making theirsel's redeclus in the eyes of everybody and trigging theirsel's out in a manner that is a shame to be zeed? You tells about women docters and women lawyers and women this, that and t'other. Who wants 'em fer gudeness saake?

Do you mean to tell me if I was sick-an'-bad in bed I should want a wumman doctor itemming about? 'Tid'n nice thing, fer a start. And 'tidn a nice thing fer any dacent body to come yer and talk about in public. And women lawyers! Why do 'em zeek to be lawyers? Simply cus they'm anxious to go poking their noses in other volks' business. Better-fit they'd bide to washtub and larn the way to cook anybody's grub proper, and sew the buttons on a body's shurt. Tell about being aiqual to men. I wish to gudeness they'd try to be the aiqual to what the women was in days gone by, when they knowed the way to hannle a scrubbing-brish, or wad'n above picking stones in the vields, and could vind jobs nuff about the houze to last 'em till time to go to bed. Anybody could live with 'em then. And knowed where to vind 'em to, when they was wanted. But now, begad, you never knaws where they'm gwain to next, nor what they'm gwain to be up to.

'The way the women be gwain on now-a-days, and the stoobid ole crams they gets in their minds, they'm no more gude about the houze then a gale o' wind; and about as aisy to manage. 'Tis a very wrong thing, in my estimation, you putting these maze-crack idayas into the heads o' maidens, and giving 'em a paasel of fanciful notions above the station they was ordained fer to occupy. There'll be a jidgment come upon 'em bim-by, you mark my words, and more pa'ticly on they what be incouraging of 'em.

'You tell about women-volk working on the land aiqual to men. 'Tis lies and desate. I knaw, cus I had one of 'em, back when the war was on. They axed me to employ Poll Bradferd's maid, and so I did, cus I thought 'twould be charity. And what was the result o' that! Soon's ever her was axed to do a man's job her kicked up her heels and away-do-go.'

How much longer Farmer would a-went on, and what more he wude a-said I can't tell 'ee. But Poll Bradferd hap'm'd to be be back o' the rume and bevore he could utter another word her jumped up and holleyed out:

'You liard! Dare you say such things!' And her went fer'n like a pickpocket.

Poll Bradferd id'n one of the pa'ticler sort, best o' times. Her daun' matter very much what her says, nor who her says it to. And her hates the very sight of Farmer Urferd, so, o' cou'se, her got fire-'ot when he said what he did about her darter. What things her did shout at'n from the back o' the rume, to be sure. And what her couldn' think of, there was several around ready to help her with. Not that her wanted very much assistance, come to that.

Everybody in the rume jumped around to zee the ole dumman, and cheerman was up in a minute to bring her to order, as the saying is. But the man what cude stop Poll Bradferd's tongue id'n born yet. Poor Jim Bradferd died in the attemp', long ago.

'I must ax Mrs. Bradferd to abide by the rules,' the passen baaled out, top of his voice. 'I shall call upon her to spaik in her turn.'

'I don't want nobody to call upon me to spaik,' her says. 'I can spaik without any calling upon. I shude think I've had calling enough, I dunnaw what you think. And raycalling, too. How ever that there ole man Urferd have got the faace to stand there and tell up sitch lies is a marvel to me. 'Tis a wonder he ab'm bin struck daid. Took my maid out o'charity did he? Who's charity was it? 'Twad'n no charity to me, that's fer certin, and 'twad'n no charity to the maid. 'Twas charity to hiszelf, that's all, same's it alwis is with he. 'Tis no gude you pulling faaces to me,' her says to the cheerman, 'and 'tis no gude you making meanings fer me to zit down, cus I shall zit down when I've said what I've got to say, and not bevore. You did'n prevent him from radiculing me, and you ban't gwain to stop me from spaiking up on behalf of my awn flesh and blid. He says my maid jacked up the job cus her was axed to prevorm a man's work. 'Tis 'bominable lies; and that's without any baiting about the bush. Her's a better man then he ever was or ever will be, and her done a sight more work than ever he'd have the faace to ax a man to do, fer all he've got the chick of the Ole Nick. But what he wanted was a man's work fer a cheel's pay. All through the week 'twas, 'I shall expec' you do this, and I shall expec' you to do that.' But when come Zaturdy night, 'twas a differnt tale. 'Twas, 'O' cou'se, you waun' expec' to receive a man's wage. If I gives 'ee vive shullin's you ought to be very well plaised.'

'That's the manner of aiquality ole man Urferd would like, and a gude many more the zame. Aiquality of work and quarter the money. That 'ud suit he fine, but it don't suit everybody. And in future I should advise he not to open his mouthe hardly so wide about my maid, else he'll have to yer the truth from me. And the truth don't suit everybody, speshly they what ab'm got very much use for it theirsel's. That's all I've got to say and I've said it, and they what daun' like it can do t'other thing.'

I'm bothered if that did'n purt'-near putt 'paid' to the Littery

Society. When Poll Bradferd sot down twenty volk started talking to-once, one across t'other. Some was in favour of Poll and reckoned what her said was no more than truth; and others was agin her, and said her ought to be ashamed of herzel'; but not loud nuff fer her to hear 'em, cus they knowed her was quite capable of letting off another such lot. To make matters worse Farmer Urferd stood up and started answering back Mrs. Bradferd. Up jumps the cheerman. 'You muzzen spaik again, Mr. Urferd. The rules is that each body must only spaik once.'

'What about you?' says Farmer. 'You keeps on cheeming in.'

'I be cheerman,' says paasen, 'and 'tis my juty to zee that the rules is abide by. We would now like to year Mr. Peter Rowe.'

That was artful move, cus Peter's a eddicative sort o' chap and he made a very gude spaich fer they what could grasp the meaning aw't. But it got 'em quiet, and arter that I dersay everything wude a-went as right as two ninepences if that-there stoobid Lias Buzzacott had'n putt in his spoke, and upzet the whole applecart. Soon as ever Lias stood up us knowed very well to look out fer zummin vulish.

'You say,' says Lias, 'is women the aiqual to men? Why, of course they be and a gude deal more so. Show me the man what can keep up-sides with a wumman. I should like to zee 'en. I never zeed one yet that could. I never couldn'. There's some as thinks they can, but that's cus they never tried. Wait till they gets one o' their awn, then they'll very soon change their mind. That's why I never married none aw'm, cus I knawed her'd get the better o' me every time.'

'Cou'se, by this time 'most everybody in the rume was roaring laafing, speshly they at the back. And Lizbeth Aish 'olleyed out, 'Nobody wouldn' have 'ee, that's why you never got married.'

'Aw, wouldn' 'um?' says Lias. 'What about you? You tried hard nuff to get me, did'n 'ee?'

That sot 'em all properly scritching. Cheerman done his best to call 'em to order, and ringed his bell, but 'twad'n a bit o' gude. 'Twas gone too fur, and there was too many anxious to yer what Lias would say next.

'Tell about women aiqual to men,' he says. 'I cude name 'ee a dizzen men, yer in this rume, what id'n the aiqual to their wives not by long chalks.' Then he cast his eye around the rume, to pick 'em out. And they knowed he'd got the chick to do it too, so there was a middling vine upstore, you mid be sure. The married men was shaking in their shoes, and trying not to ketch Lias's eye. And the zingle young chaps was jumping up and pointing out differnt ones which they thought would suit Lias's purpose. And all the committee as white as a sheet, 'sep the squire, who was trying to pretend he wad'n injoying it.

Paasen he jumped right up top of his cheer with his bell in his hand ringing like houze a-vire.

'There muzzen be no naming of names,' he says. ''Tis agin the rules.'

'That's all right, yer 'onner,' says Lias. 'I ban't gwain to name no names. There id'n no need for that. You've only got to look around the rume and you can pick 'em out fer yerzel.' There's thik poor li'l feller sot back there in the corner without a word to say fer hiszel.' He use to . . .'

My gudeness gracious! What Lias said else I can't tell 'ee, there was sitch a rumpus in the plaace. Of cou'se, everybody turned around to look to Jimmy Quant. He'm only a li'l bit of a chap, and when he married Jane Godbeer her was about three times his size, and her've gone on increasing ever since. Years agone Jimmy use to have as much to say as any two ord'nery chaps, but latterly he ab'm bin able to get a word in sideways, so he've sorter got out o' the way of it, like.

But Mrs. Quant her's perfec'ly capable to do Jimmy's share and her awn besides, her up and went fer Lias like wile-fire. That jis' plaised Lias, you mid depaind, and there was they two yapping one across t'other, and the rest o' the volks at the back fulling up the gaps, as you mid say.

I tell 'ee 'twas proper pandemonian there fer a bit, and Mrs. Jinkins looking daggers cus her butiful spaich was all ruined, and cheerman knocking his ole bell like Tom Rogers cracking stones.

And to-last he rised up and said the debate was all over. But 'twad'n, cus arter they'd cleared all the volks out o' the rume you could yer it gwain on in the strate fer howers.

Some people will tell 'ee that our Littery Society wad'n a success. But I've yeard a-plenty say that they've paid money before now to go into intertaments and did'n get half-quarter the injoyment.

NED HANNAFORD KEEPS HOUSE

About a man who welcomed the opportunity of showing his wife that he could do her household duties 'on his head.' Ned Hannaford is the village carpenter and wheelwright.

Ned Annaferd told two differnt tales. This is the fus' one, which he praiched up one day in the Carrier's Cart.

'Why is it,' he says, 'that women gets the idaya that men be all gawks about the houze, and can't manage to look after theirsel's if they'm left alone?'

'Why is it, I wonder,' says Mrs. Snell. 'Must be zome raison, for it, fer certin.'

'Aw, you thinks it too, seem-so,'

'No, I don't think it, I knows it,' her says. 'Men-volk be all right to their own jobs, I derzay. But about the houze they ab'm got no more gumtion than a cat.'

"Tid'n true,' says Ned. "Tis only a stoobid ole cram that the women has got in their mind. My wive have been praiching up that yarn to me fer years, but I tells her 'tis all rummage. I'll make a bet I'd do all the work there in a houze on me haid.'

'I'll warran' you would, Mr. Annaferd,' says Mrs. Snell. 'And that's just about how it would look, arter you'd vinished.'

'Daun' you believe it,' he saith. 'I'll tell you the whole truth o' the matter, missis. The women-volk railizes that any fule could undertake their job, but they daun' want it to be generally knowed, and so they thinks if they keeps on telling about what a tremenjis lot they've got to do, and what difficult job 'tis to do it proper, the volks will come to believe it in the end. Matter o' fac', they've said it so many times that they've come to believe it theirsel's.'

When I yeard Ned talking that fashin, I thought to mezel', 'There's more behind this than the eye can zee.' So I said:

'Have you been discussing the subjic' with your missis, Ned?'

94

'Yes, I have, Jan,' he says.

'I thought whether you had'n or no. Did you want to change jobs with her, or what?'

"Twad'n that, zac'ly,' he saith. 'But my wive ordains gwain away fer a vew days on a visit to her sister, down about Tiverton. And the fuss and bother her was making, about what I should do while her was gone, and how I should manage to look after mezel,' you'd a-thought I was a cheel about vive year old.'

'"Gude gracious me," I says. "Do 'ee think I can't look after the plaace fer a day or two, and get a vew meals?"

'"You waun' need to bother about nothing o' that," her says. "I've arranged fer Anna Loosemore to come and manage everything."

'"I daun zee what you want to do that for," I says. "I daun' want that ole wumman furraging about yer. I can very well zee to all there is to be done while you'm away, and do me own work same time."

'"Daun' you be vulish," her says. "If I thought you was gwain messing about the plaace I wouldn' go."

'"No," I thought to mezel', "cus if I was to do, it would prove that there id'n nothing so very wonderful about it, and that's the very thing you'm 'fraid of."'

That was Ned's fus' tale.

A vortnit arterwards us was all in the Carrier's Cart again. Somehow, Ned zeemed a lot more quieter than usual.

'Ban't 'ee veeling up to the mark, Mr. Annaferd?' says Mrs. Snell.

'I be all right, thank you, missis,' he says. 'What makes 'ee think otherwise?'

'I dunnaw,' her says. 'Only you'm sot there so mum-chance, I thought p'r'aps you was veeling quare-like.'

'That id'n nothing to go by,' he says. "Tis only the women that be always talking.'

'Have Mrs. Annaferd returned back 'ome yet, Ned?' I says.

'Yes, Jan, her's back 'ome again,' he says, trying to look as if he did'n matter whether her was back or no. But I hap'm'd to know a bit more than he give me credic for, cus I'd yeard a thing or two.

'How did 'ee get on with the 'ouze-keeping, then? Orright?'

'Middling.'

'Gwain to take it on for gude?'

Ned laafed. 'No, I ban't gwain to take it on for gude,' he says. 'And I ban't gwain to take it on for bad, nuther. I spause I

95

mid-so-well tell the truth bout it, cus if I daun't you will.'

'Did 'ee find that any fule could do it, Mr. Annaferd?' says Mrs. Endycott.

'No, I did'n, missis. I found one fule what could'n. I'll take back all I said a vortnit agone.

'I told 'ee that my missis had bespoke ole Anna Loosemore to come up every day and zee to things. Wull, the very day mother left, Anna was tooked bad with the brownkittis, and her chubes was chucked to that extaint her never got up out o' bed fer a week. Her sent a message to say her could get Poll Bradferd to come in her place if I wude wish it.

'So I thought to mezel', "This have all turned out fer the best, and I waun' have nobody, and then I can let my missis see that 'tid'n no gurt criterion to do up a few chores and get a bit o' grub. So I told Anna to never mind, cus I'd arranged everything myzelf.

"'Twas Mondy, middle day, when the missis went away, and her'd left plenty grub provided to last out the rest o' the day, so there wad'n nothing very much to bother about. As you do knaw, us have got the three li'l chillern 'o my sister Bessie that died; that's the oldest maid jis turned nine, and the nex' one zix,, and the li'l tacker rising vower. There was they three to zee to; and my two chaps what works in the shop, they comes in fer meals. But I did'n zee no difficulty about that.

'Wull, eveything went off that day as suant as graise, and I thought to mezel', "I can't zee where the women have got so much to create about. 'Tis cheel's play."'

'Nothing had'n been left to doing,' says Mrs. Snell.

'Stop a minute,' says Ned. 'Well, nex' morning I sot up in bed and thought to mezel.' "Now, let's zee what is to be done. There's the brekfus to be got and the chillern to zend off to skule, then tidy up a bit, and zee to the dinner. Couple howers will do the lot, and then I can get on with painting Mr. Tucker's cart, cus I wants that out the way."

'So I'ops out o' bed and went down over stairs.

'"Now," I says to mezel,' "fus' thing light up a bit o' vire and putt on a kettle o' watter." Zo I tooked in a vew sticks and started the vire gwain and then I carr'd the kettle out to the pump. That putt me in the mind that the hens mus' be fed, so I went an' got they a bit o' corn. By that time, me vire had gone out.

'"I'll soon stop your li'l caper," I says, and I took the belisses to 'en. But the sticks was a bit green, and I'm darned if I cude get'n to go as

96

I wished. He'd blaze away all right while I was blowing to 'en, but soon's I stopped he'd stop. 'Twas turrifying to have to bide there wasting yer time when there was other things wanted attending to. So to-last I goes out in shop and cut up a bit o' dry 'ood and then I very soon had the vire roaring up the chumley.

'By thees time the chillern was down. '"Twaun' be very long bevore you gets yer brekfus," I says. '"I've got a gude vire gwain."'

'"Why daun' 'ee putt the kettle on, uncle?" says li'l Bessie.

'My, jaly! All that lovely vire burned away and nothing in it. "Rin and get the kettle, my dear," I says.

'Wull, then nobody couldn' vind the kettle. "Jus' like the women," I says. "Why daun' 'em have a proper plaace fer everything? That's how they makes so much extry work."

'And with the zame I remembered I'd carr'd out the kettle to the pump and lef' 'n there when I fed the chickens. So while the chillern was seeking in another derection I went out and took'n in.

'By that time I had to make up me vire again. I dunnaw what was the matter with 'n, but every time I turned me back on 'en, the blimming thing went out. However, I made the kettle boil, to-last. Matter o' fac', he boiled when I was laist expecting, and you can zee the marks on me hands now, where the bladders was to.

'Zeeing the watter boiling putt me in the mind o' the tay-pot. I intended having he down by the vire bevorehand, to get 'ot, cus I reckon you makes better tay that way. But with so many things to think about it went out o' me head. However. I vound the tay-pot and I putt in zeb'm spunes o' tay. That was one each a-piece and one fer the pot. I knowed the rules, you zee. Then I beginned to zee about summin to ait.'

'Must a-bin a rare dish o' tay, time you was raddy fer't,' says Mrs. Snell.

'And so you wude have said, if you'd had to drink it,' says Ned. 'Be-as-'twill, I knowed the chillern was in the habit of having this-yer porridge trade, and I did'n reckon there could be very much in doing that. I wad'n quite certin which way to go to work, but the derections was on the packet, so I couldn' go very fur wrong, fer certin. I measured out the proper quantity into a sasspan and rest it on the vire, and then I sot about putting the things on the taable. 'Tis very important that anybody should be able to keep two or dree jobs gwain to-once, so's not to waste time. But 'tis a beggar to knaw when you've got everything on the taable, and while I was glimpsing around to zee what else was required I yeard a fizzing noise behind; and that was the porridge boiling out over. Wull, I made a dive to save as much as possible, but the hannle o' the sasspan was rid-'ot, and I let'n go a lot quicker'n I took 'n up, and said zummat which I daun' usually bevore the chillern. Sasspan turned up-an-down, and the whole lot o' the porridge went on the vire. So that was the end o' that.

'"Never mind," I says, "you can do wi'out porridge to-day and have double quanity to-morra." 'Twas getting laate, and time the chaps was called in to brekfus. I was frightend to zee how the time had gone. 'Tis wonderful how it do flip along when you got a-plenty to do.

'Wull, nex' thing was to fry the baacon an' aigs. But I did'n reckon that would be any trouble. And 'twude'n a-bin very much if everything had'n tried to be as ockerd as posible. Fer one thing, 'tid'n aisy to tell when the baacon have had cooking enough. Once or twice I was in two minds about taking it out o' the pan, but I thought I'd give it one more frizzle to make sure. By the time I did take it out 'twas like a han'ful o' chips. And then I had'n got no plaace to rest it to, cus I'd fergot about putting plaates down to yetty. So I had to putt it on the cold plaates and rest 'em down bevore the vire. 'Twad'n very long bevore they was smothered in aishes.

'"Never mind," I says. "Whoever eats most baacon must eat most grit. And the docters all say us ought to eat more grit."

'Then I tooked the aigs and cracked 'em open on the zide o' the pan, same's mother do. Or 'twas intainded to be the zame, but I hat the fust one a bit hard and he went plop in the vire, and left the shell in me hand. I reckon I must a-bin a bit too aiger. The nex' one I squaished right up in me vist. However, what there was of it did go in the pan, so 'twad'n what you might call wasted, if anybody mind to pick out the bits o' shell. Only one out o' the whole lot went in proper. The rest was all to a huh! But I vried it and zot it on the taable.

The chaps was in and sot down by thees time. But George said he wad'n very pa'ticler about brekfus, cus he wad'n veeling very well. And Wi'yum said he had his brekfus that morning avore he left 'ome. The chillern said they'd sooner have a slishe o' bread 'n jam. So I could have eat the lot if I'd bin mind to; only I daun' fancy you veels like eating very much arter you've cooked it yerzel.'

'I waun' go so fur as to say the brekfus was a gurt success. I dersay there wude a-bin plenty glad to eat it, but they'd need to be sight more hungerd than what us was. I must admit, you couldn' tell fer certin which was aigs and which was baacon and which was aishes. 'Twas almost what you might call a ommylick. Only to look at the colour you'd a-thought the whole lot must a-come down the chumley.

'"Never mind," I says, '"twill be better nex' time. I had'n hardly got me hand in."

'"I should think you must a-got yer foot in, bevore you clained yer butes," says George.

'"'Twis only the colour is a bit dark," I says. "The taste is all right, you may depaind,"

'George said he'd take my word for it. And Wi'yum said he would, too.

'"Wull, you chillern rin along to skule," I says, "and I'll have a nice dinner all ready fer 'ee on the taable when you comes 'ome. You chaps mix up a bit o' paint and have everything ready to finish off Mr. Tucker's cart. I'll be along in a jiffy."

'So they all cleared off and lef' me to it. I reckoned about half-nower would zee everything straight.

'"Whatever a wumman can vind to go pottering about all the morning, I can't think," I said to mezel.'

Fust wash up the brekfus things and putt they away. That waun' take vive minutes. Caw, darn 'ee! Shall want 'ot watter fer that. Ought to have had the watter on to boil while us was having brekfus! Never mind, waun' take a minute.'

'But my darned ole vire had gone daid again, so I had to make he up fresh. And then I fulled up the kettle and hanged he up to the crook. I putt up the dish with the baacon and the rest aw't down fer the dog. I'm blowed if he did'n think twice about it. But I spause he considered 'twas that or nort, so he turned to and eat it. So that dish was half washed avore I come to it. I carr'd out all the durty platters and things to the back-'ouze where I'd zeed mother wash 'em up to, but thik kettle tooked a doost of a time to boil. I should think there must a-bin a frog in 'en.

'"Muzzen poke about doing nort," I says. "While I be waiting fer the watter I'll run the brish over the kitchen floor."

'But when I come to look, they two chaps had carr'd in so much muck on their butes, 'twas useless to think about sweeping it up with the brish. I knowed my missis wouldn' leave the floor in that pickle, so I thought I'd run over it with a drap o' watter. 'Twouldn' take a minute.

'So I tooked in a bucket o' watter, and furraged about fer a clath and a scrubbing-brish and a bit o' zope, and down I goes on me marra-bones.

'"Women-volk makes a diggins of a scummer about scrubbing up a floor," I says too mezel.' "I'll let 'em zee how *I* should do it."

'So I emp' a-plenty o' water out o' the bucket on the floor, cus I orwis think the women skimps the watter too much on they jobs. I'll admit I empt out a bit more'n I intainded, and that minute the ole kettle boiled over. Do I left me scrubbing and carr'd on with the washin'-up.

'I got over thik job orright, although it takes anybody longer than they'd think. Every time you reckons you've done the last thing you looks around and zees another left to doing. And I wad'n sure fer certin which was the right clath fer drying 'em. Missis tole me arterwards that I used the dister, but it answered the purpose all right.

'I had a bit of a mis'ap over thik job, although, o' cou'se, that might hap'm to anybody. When I'd vinished wiping the things dry I had to carr' 'em into the bes' kitchen. Really spaiking, I ought to have took 'em to-twice, but I thought 'twould zave time if I stacked 'em up on the big dish and tooked 'em all to-once. But there's a li'l bit of a stap to go up, and I 'itched me voot in he, and the sudden jerk overbalanced the top lot and down they went, wollop. Dree tay-cups and two tay-sassers scat all abroad to shords.

'"Twad'n my fau't, mind. If thik old stap ad'n bin in the way, it would never have hap'm'd. However, I did'n zee no call to make a zong about it, and I knowed I could replace the cups and sassers into Barleycombe so I buried the shords out in back garden, cus what the eye daun' zee the 'art daun' grieve about.'

'And did Mrs. Annaferd never vind ''ee out?' says Mrs. Endycott.

'Her never wouldn' a-done,' says Ned, 'if the cat had'n went and had kittens.'

'Whatever nonsainse be you telling about now?'

'Well, you zee mother drownded three o' they kittens and buried 'em out in garden. And I'm jiggered if her did'n choose the very spot where the shords was to.'

'Well, get on with yer houze-keeping,' says Mrs. Snell. 'I wants to yer the rest.'

'There wad'n no rest,' says Ned. 'Not fer me, anyrate. When I went back to me floor I vound that the watter which I'd left there had trickled in under the buroo, and in under the long-sleeve clock and I had to shift out all the furniture to dry up the mess. I never intainded to more than wash down the middle, but now I had to go all in around the sides. And I'm beggered if that daun' take anybody a time. I'd keep on taking in another fresh bit and another fresh bit, and I'd think it mus' be nearly all vinished, and when I lookid around I couldn' hardly zee what I'd done.'

'I fancy I've yerd you making sport o' your wive fer using they very words.' says Mrs. Snell.

'I dersay you have, missis,' says Ned. 'But I doubt if you ever will again. However, in the middle of it all in comes George to say they was ready fer me to go on with Mr. Tucker's cart.

' "I'll be there in two shakes, George," I says. "You can let it bide 'fore I come, and you and Wi'yum go on with they pigs'-traws fer the squire, and get they out o' the way."

'But I'm jiggered if I wad'n frightened to zee the time when I'd finished washing the floor. No gude thinking about gwain out in shop. If I did'n start on with the dinner purty quick, nothing wouldn' be ready fer the chillern when they come 'ome from skule.

'I zeed a couple o' rabbuts hanged up, and I reckoned they was intainded fer Anna Loosemore to cook. But I considered I could cook a couple o' rabbuts as well as what Anna Loosemore could. Better per'aps. There wad'n very much in cooking a rabbut, fer certin. 'I shall want the oven hot fer that,' I thought to mezel.' That meant lighting up a vire in the stove. I ought to a-done that sooner so's it could be getting hot. However, better late than never.

'But lighting up the ole stove wad'n quarter so aisy as making a vire on the hearth. 'Twas a turk of a job to get'n to go, and I had the plaace chuck-ful o' smoak bevore I could vind out which o' they ole damper things I mus' pull out and which I mus' push in. I tried 'em all ways. However, I got'n in the mind to go, to-last, but o' cou'se, the oven was cold as a stoan. "Never mind," I thought to mezel,' "he'll be hot by the time I be ready fer 'en. I'll prepare they rabbuts now."

'Fust of all the skeen must be took off.'

'Aw, you knowed that much then?' says Mrs. Snell.

'Yes, I knowed that much. I never had'n acshally skeened a rabbut bevore, but I'd zeed it done scores o' times, and I 'lowed there wad'n very much in it. But I'm blowed if there id'n a gurt difference in looking on to other volks doing a job and doing it yerzel.' By gude right, that skeen should have come off as aisy as

101

taking off a glove. But I might all-so-well try to pull the whiskers off a billy-goat. I wad'n zac'ly sure where you was supposed to start to, but whichever end I tried I did'n make very much of a vist aw't.

'So I carr'd 'em out in shop, to zee whether my chaps knowed anything about it. But they wad'n much better than me. However, George said, "You give me hold to the rabbut, maister, and you hang on to the skeen and us'll both pull to 'en. Zummat must go, fer certin."

'So us done that. Us managed to get 'em apart, but 'twas question which had the most rabbut.

'"Which be gwain to cook, maister," says George, "the rabbut or the skeen?"

'"Us'll try t'other rabbut," I says. "P'r'aps he'll be more raisonable."

'He was, a bit, but not a lot. They looked like as if the cat had bin at 'em.

'"Never mind," I says, "they'll be all the zame when they'm cooked."

'"I shouldn' be surprised, maister," says George. I had a good mind to ax him what he meant, but I was feared he might tell me.

'I putt what was left o' the rabbuts into a tin dish and sticked 'em in the oven, very glad to zee the back of 'em. "Now," I says, "while you'm baking I'll zee about skinning a few tetties. I reckon I can manage that, if I can't skeen a rabbut."

'But laur, tayjus ole job that is, paring tetties, and takes anybody a lot longer than they'd think. Time I'd vinished thik job I considered the rabbuts ought to be looking a bit dinnerified, zo I opened the oven and glimpsed inzide. They did'n look to me a scrap differnt to when I putt 'em in, and the oven wad'n hot nuff to melt a spit o' butter. What was the matter wai't I can't tell 'ee; but I spause I'd done zummin I did'n ought to a-done, or left undone zummin I shude a-done, or zummin. Be-as-'twill, there 'twas. They had'n begun to yetty.

'"Caw, darn 'ee!" I says, "if you waun' roastee you must boilee, that's all."

'Time was getting short, so I hoiked 'em out and cut 'em up in li'l bits and shoved 'em all in a pot, tetties and all with a-plenty o' watter, and putt the pot on the vire. "Now you can boil to yer heart's containt," I says.

'Tell 'ee straight, by that time I was veeling a bit wicked, cus everything zeem determined to go as contr'y as possible. 'Twas a

diggins of a time bevore the ole pot wude boil at all. If I tooked off
the lid to look once, I did vorty times; and I blowed the ole vire till I
purt' near bust the bellisses.

'However, he did boil to-last, and zoon arter that the chillern and
the chaps come in to dinner. So I turned the whole lot out in a gurt
dish and putt it on the taable. I zeed George give a gude look at it.

'"What's think aw't?" I says.

'"I was jis' thinking, maister," he says, "us have finished they
pigs'-traws zac'ly right time."

'"You'll vind 'tis better'n it looks," I says.

'"I'll make a bet it is," he says. "It cude'n be otherwise."

'But when I come to try it, I wad'n hardly so sure.

"Twad'n exac'ly what you'd call a jovial party, sot around the
dinner-taable. As a rule my chaps is jokified and carr'ing on with
paasel of ole items, and the chillern is full o' their antics, and
everybody yapping one across t'other. That's when mother cooks
the dinner.

'But this time 'twas more as though us had a corpse upstairs.
Chaps had'n got a word to say, and the chillern looked more like as
if they'd start to cry fer two peens. I thought 'twad'n very polite of
'em arter a body had gived up all the morning, same's I had, and
done his best fer 'em, and then fer they to turn sulky.

'Mind you, I ban't gwain to say that rabbut stew looked hardly so
tem'ting to the naked eye as what anybody might wish; and the
smell wad'n sufficient to make 'ee eat whether you was hungerd or
no. But there was no call fer George to ax whether I'd got it mixed
up with the week's wash. Nor yet fer Wi'yum to remark that he
hoped he wad'n depriving the ole zow.

'"I'll make a bet you eat wiss than that when you was sawjering,"
I says.

'"Yas," says George, "but I got a medal fer that."

'"Wull you try it," I says, "and zee if it id'n better'n you thinks."

'"Spause you tries it fust, maister, and then if nothing daun'
hap'm to you us'll know 'tid'n so bad as it looks."

'"Aw, don't you make no error," I says. "I be gwain to ait my
share and injoy it."

'Zo I fulled up all the platters and tooked a gude dollop fer mezel'.'

'You was determined to eat it if it killed 'ee?' says Mrs. Endycott.

'That's about it, missis. And between you and me and the
gate-paust, that's purt' near what it did do. Mind, I daun' say but

103

what it might a-bin all right if I'd putt in a bit o' zalt and pipper, and a li'l vat baacon and vew things like o' that. Or if I'd let it boil long nuff to get the rabbut cooked it mightn' a-bin so bad. But you cude'n says he was properly hot, not right in through; so 'twas like a tay-spoonful o' gin in a jugful o' watter, neether one thing ner t'other. I tried me hardest to eat it, to set example to the rest, but, 'pon me zaul, 'twas more'n I cude stommick. And o' cou'se, they was all watching me.

'"How do he go, maister?" says George.

'"Aw, not so bad," I says. "Rabbut's a bit tow. Must a-bin old ones."

'"Old nuff to knaw better, I should think" says George.

'"Have some bread and mix up with the braath," I says, "you'll like it that way."

'"Why, what's the matter with the bread?" he says. "You did'n make that as well, did 'ee?"

'"Daun' you be redeclus," I says. "Bread's very nice in the gravy."

'"I'd sooner have it as 'tis," he says.

'"You dunnaw what 'tis like yet," I says. "You ab'm tried it."

'"No," he says, "but I've bin watching your faace."

'"Wull," I says, "what do 'ee think us better do with it?"

'"What, your faace?"

'"No, stoobid; the stew."

'"Tell 'ee what I thinks ought to do with it, maister," says Wi'yum. "I should putt it back in pot again, and let it boilee fer another hower or two and then give it to the ducks. Ducks is the laist pa'ticler things on the farm of what they eats."

'"Look yer, you chaps," I says, "I've had about nuff o' your sass. 'Tis like yer chick, I reckon. Yer have I been and give up all the blessid morning trying to do me best to give 'ee a nice dinner, and I daun' zee why you wants to turn up yer nose at'n vor."

'"Us daun' want to turn 'en up, maister," says George. "Us wants to stap 'en up."

'"You'm too taffity, be-half," I says. "When I was your age I'd have jumped to a dinner like that."

'"I shouldn' be 't all surprised," says George. "Purt' near made me jump, mezel'.'

'"I spause you thinks that's clivver," I says, "but 'tid'n. 'Tis only daft; and sassy 'pon tap o' that. If you was hungerd you could eat yer dinner, and if you ban't hungerd then 'tid'n no odds whether you eats it or no."

'I tell 'ee, I was properly narked, what with one thing and another, and the way everything had went wrong, and so I spoke out a bit sharp-like. But George was out-to-end with he's patience, too, and I'm darned if he did'n spaik out likewise.

'"Let me tell 'ee, maister," he says, "that you'm wrong. I *be* hungerd. I ab'm had no brekfus, cus what you putt to the taable 's-morning the cat wude'n eat; and I've bin working hard all the vorenoon, as you can zee fer yerzel' if you mind to come out and look. And now I be properly leery; but I cude'n stommick thik ole trade. I wouldn' give it belly-rume, and that's telling of 'ee straight. And I'll tell 'ee zummat else, Mr. Annaferd, while us be about it. You'm a very gude weel-wright and you'm a very gude boss. Nobody cude'n wish fer better. But you'm a darn poor cook; and if you daun' know it you ought to be told; and now yu've *been* told. And if I've got to have the sack fer telling 'ee, well, so 'tis."'

'Quite right, too,' says Mrs. Snell. 'I daun' blame the feller fer spaiking up like it.'

'Right?' says Ned. 'Of course 'twas right. And arter I'd lookid the feller straight in the faace fer a minute or two I ketched up the dish o' rabbut stew and emp' the whole lot out o' winder.

'And then George he laafed, and Wi'yum he laafed, and the chillern they laafed, and the dog beginned to bark, and the cat putt up his back and spit, and went out the winder arter the rabbut. And then us all had another laaf, and that putt our tempers to rights, like a thinder-storm will clear the air.

'"I'm darned if you ab'm told the truth fer once, George," I said. "I wad'n cut out fer a cook, or else I did'n start young enough or zummin. But the question is, what us be gwain to have to eat."

'"Let's have a bit o' bread and chaise, maister, and pickle' ingyen," he says. '"Twill keep a body from starving, anyway."

'"Can't us do no better'n that?" I says. "That id'n very much of a dinner."

'"'Tis bevore rabbut-stew," he says.

'"There's thik 'em what auntie lef' in the larder," says the oldest maid, "and there's aigs you cude boil if you mind to."

'I opened me eyes and stared to the cheel. You've got to open 'em middling wide, for her id'n much higher than a hand-zaw.

'"Go and have a glimpse around, my dear," I says, "and zee what you can vind. I had'n sainse nuff too look and zee what was in the larder."

'So her went furraging around, and vound no end o' things which my wive had left behind in raddiness, and which, o' cou'se, ole Anna would have dished up if her'd bin there. Her tooked out a butiful new pie, never bin titched, and lovely bit of 'am, and tomaters and I dummaw what-all.

'"Corn in Aigyp',' I says. "Us can make a very gude meal off o' thik pie. Pity 'twad'n hot, though."

'"If you mind to hav'n hot, uncle," says li'l Bessie, "you could have zome 'am and a boiled aig now, and hot up the pie fer zupper. Then George and Wi'yum could have a nice feed avore they goes home."

'"Whatever putt that idaya into yer haid?" I says.

'"Tid'n a bad idaya," says George.

'"Bad!" I says, "'tis a very gude idaya, I should think. But where did her get it to, that's what beats me. Why, her id'n much bigger than a jack-plane. But what's the use o' telling about making it hot, when the darned ole oven waun' work proper? Did'n I try it on the rabbut?"

'"You did," says George, "and then tried the rabbut on we."

'"I'll make the oven go," says li'l maid. "I'll putt the vire gwain avore I leaves fer skule and 'twill be rare an' 'ot when us comes home, and then it won't be nothing to hot up the pie."

'"What's use o' telling like that?" I says. "Drec'ly you turns yer back on the vire he'll go out."

'"No he waunt," uncle,' her says. "Not if you leaves 'n alone he waun't."

Caw! Didn't they chaps laaf! They said li'l maid had got it zac'ly. 'Guessed right fust time.' George reckoned her had.

'Wull, and then her sot about boiling they aigs, and her said her'd make a cup o' tay, cus what us had fer brekfus wad'n fit to drink.

'Wad'n fit to drink mind 'ee! The sassy li'l baggage! And I thought I made it zo butiful.

'"What do 'ee mean, not fit to drink? Did'n I putt in one fer everybody and one fer the pot?"

'"Ees, uncle," her says "and if aunt had zeed 'ee her'd have had a fit. I was vexed to zee 'ee waste the tay like it."

'Her was vexed, mind 'ee! The li'l faggit! And her scarcely abble to look over the tap o' the taable, and her was vexed! Well, if that did'n beat cock-fighting.

'And I'm jiggered if her did'n have the tay and the cups an' sassers on the taable, and the aigs and all the rest aw't, bevore you could

106

look around, hardly. And all done proper, too. No fuss, and no scummer. And darn the maid, her id'n much higher than the spokes of a wheel.

'And what her done to thik stove, or what her said to 'en, I can't tell 'ee; but in one minute he was roaring away like a train. And her went away to skule, and when her come back he was still gwain lovely. I spause her told 'n he was to. I durzen go near the blessid thing, cus I knawed if I looked at'n he'd go right out. And 'tid'n to say her's a gurt wumman. Bless yer zaul, her id'n much higher than my walking-stick. And if her did'n hot up thik pie and putt'n up to taable, fer zupper, jis' like mother would. And her id'n hardly high nuff to look in oven.

'And when the zupper was all over, her carr'd away the platters, and the hot watter was all there in raddiness, and 'twas all washed up and putt away while you was fulling up yer pipe, purt' near. Darn 'ee, and her not very much higher than the hannle o' the door.

'If it had been me I shude a-bin messing about till the middle o' the night.

'And when her'd putt everything to rights her took the other chillern and kiss me gude night and away-do-go up-over stairs to bed.

'Me and the two chaps sot on a bit, and smocked a pipe o' baccy. And arter a while, I said:

'"Men is men, and women is women."

'"Did zomebody tell 'ee that, maister?" says George, "or did you rade it in a book?"

'"Wait a bit," I says. "There's a differnce. A man id'n a man till he's full growed, but a wumman's a wumman as soon as her's abble to walk."'

THE BEAUTY SHOW

The Author was one of the judges in a 'West-country Beauty Competition' arranged by the 'Western Weekly News.' From a large number of photographs sent in ten entrants were chosen to attend at Plymouth, and from these the three judges made the final selection.

I'm bothered if I know what's the matter with me laately. I zeem to be all the time in hot watter. I be no zooner out from one ole scummer than I be into another.

It never did'n use to be like it, I daun' fancy. I use to be able to go along quiet and peaceable, and mind me own interference and nobody to trouble about me. One day same's another and Zundy once a wik.

But now begad they waun' laive me alone a minute. They'm arter me fer all manner o' things. But this darned ole Buty caper have capped the lot. That's a finisher that is. I can't think how ever I come to be so stoobid as to have anything to do wai't.

But there, 'tis orwis the zame. I be too aisy with 'em that's what's the matter. Volks axes me will I do a thing, and I goes and says, 'Yes,' wai'out thinking o' the consequences. And so I gets lured into all manner of predicaments.

And I was lured into zummat this time, I'm jiggered if I wad'n.

Not but what I could do it, mind. I waun' say but what I be as capable fer a jidge as one yer and there. 'Tid'n fust time I've been jidge to a show, not by long chalk. Fust cattle shaw ever they had to Barleycombe I was jidge o' the vat bullicks. And I was jidge o' pigs to Orcombe shaw every year till they gived it up. And when the Distric' Shaw was to Week they axed me to jidge the cart'-osses. So I reckons I knaws a bit about jidging.

But this is what you might call a differnt category, altogether. 'Tis one thing to jidge a hoss and another thing to jidge a purty maid. Not that I be feared o' the job, so fur's that's consarned. 'Tid'n that.

'Tis what have been made of it, out yer to Muddlecombe.

You zee, where the nuisance was, they went and putt my name on the paaper to say I was to be jidge in this yer buty competition. I never bargained fer that. The edditer gen'lman come to and axed me if I'd be jidge, to help pick out the purtiest maid. Well, o' cou'se, I never suspected nothing wrong. I said, 'If you thinks I can be any gude you'm quite welcome. I'll do whatever I can.'

I cude'n say no fairer than that could I? But I never throught fer a minute my name wude be exposed on the paaper.

And o' cou'se, they gawks that rides every week in the Carrier's Cart they got the news fust, cus they had the paaper up to Exeter. And they come back full aw't.

As bad luck would have it, my wive was up to Mrs. Zalter's shop arter a few arrants when Tom Zalter arrived home, and Lias Buzzacott with'n. A purty vine pair to break the news to anybody! Nice li'l paasel o' lies they told up between 'em. What one couldn' think of t'other could, zeem-zo.

Ole Tom Zalter started the ball rolling.

'Ullaw, Mrs. Stewer,' he says. 'I'm surprised at you ventering so fur away from home.'

'What ole cram be you on-upon now, Tom Zalter?' her says.

'No ole cram whatever, misses. You'd better-way bide home and keep your eye on that man o' yours. You'll be losting he, else.'

'Caw! I shude'n let that trouble me if I was you, Mr. Zalter,' her says. 'Never lost nothing that id'n no gude.'

'Wull, I dunnaw,' he says. 'If I was his missis I daun' think I should care to trist 'en among all they purty maidens.'

'What maidens, stoobid?'

'Why, this yer buty shaw, where your Jan is gwain to be jidge.'

'Ees, I'm sure,' her saith. 'I should like to ketch 'n.'

'Aw, 'tis right nuff,' says Lias. 'Yer 'tis all down in print. You can zee it fer yerzel.'

So then they shawed my wive all the whole rigmarole. Her was properly took back.

'The mump-'aided gurt gawk,' he saith. 'What ever shall us see next? Have he gone mazed or what? A purty vine jidge! I wouldn' let'n jidge a cat.'

'Everybody daun' think same's you do, fer certin,' says Lias. 'You mus' remember Jan have bin getting about a lot lately, and you mid depaind he've left his repitation behind.'

109

Ann couldn' size it up at all, zeem-zo, and her raid it down over two or dree times to try to sainse it.

'You mean to tell me,' her saith, 'that Jan have got sufficient gumtion to pick out which is purtiest of they picshers.'

'Grammer, picshers!' says Tom. 'He ab'm got to jidge the picshers. He've got to witness the acshal maidens and choose the one he considers is the 'ansummest.'

'I'll explain how 'tis done, missis,' says Lias (the lying ozeburd, that ever I should say jis-thing). ''Tis like this-yer. We'll say fer argyment sake there's three-hunderd maidens goes in fer this-yer competition. I dersay 'tis a lot more'n that really, but us'll say three-hunderd. There's three jidges, so that's a hunderd a-piece. Well, Jan's hunderd will have to come out yer to Muddlecombe, and he'll have a gude look at all of 'em, and selec' the one he thinks is the purtiest. The other jidges will do the zame down Plymouth, or wherever 'tis to, and then, bim-by they'll putt they three maidens together and decide 'em in order of fus', second an' third. That's all 'tis.'

I suppaus by all accounts my Ann's faace must a-bin a picsher.

'All!' her says. 'All, do 'ee call it? And do you think, or do anybody in his sainses think that I be gwain to have a hunderd strange maidens trapesing about my plaace? I should like to zee 'em.'

'Aw, not a hunderd all-to-once,' says Lias. 'He do's it to-twice, or as many times as necessary. He'll have out, say, ten or a dizzen one day and choose the best o' they, and then zome more the nex' day, and zo on, as long as they last out.'

'Aw, will 'er?'

''Twill be a nice li'l change fer 'ee,' says Tom, 'and intresting to the parrish as well, cus they maidens will sure to want to look about a bit while they'm yer, and view the church and sitch like.'

'All you'll have to do, missis,' says Lias, 'will be to invite 'em in and give 'em a cup o' tay and so forth, and make 'em veel 'omely, so's they shall be looking their best.'

But by that time I suppaus my wive had left. Her went out the shop, so Tom said, like a worldwind. Her come right straight home to me without hesitating, and started cracking off nineteen to the dizzen. I couldn' make out whatever her was telling about fer a bit.

'You fetch a dizzen o' the huzzies to my door,' her says. 'Or even one. I'll give 'ee Buty Shaw, I will. I'll shaw the buties the end o' the

110

sweeping-brish. I'll empt' o' bucket o' watter over the lot aw'm, jidge an' all, so I warn 'ee.'

Arter a bit, when her breath begin to rin short, I got a word in edgeways.

'I should a-thought,' I said, 'that you'd a-knowed Tom Zalter and Lias Buzzacott well 'nuff by thees time not to be had so aisy as that.'

So then I explained things a bit, and her said, 'Well, I did'n believe it when they told me; but I thought I'd better-way come and let 'ee knaw what things was being said about 'ee.'

But of cou'se, Tom and Lias carr'd it all up to the Black Oss, and shawed everybody my name on the paaper, and told up a purty vine ole ditty. So very soon 'twas all over the parrish. I hap'm'd to look into the Black Oss same aiv'min and there was the usual party sot around with Tom Zalter in the middle.

'Come on, Jan,' he said, 'us be waiting fer 'ee to pick out the purtiest.'

'That's very aisy done,' I says. 'If 'twas to pick out the ugliest twude be a bit of a job, cus you'm one so-bad as the other. But if 'tis to be the bes' looking amongs' 'ee, I should give the fus' prize to Jim Pearcey's spaniel-dog there.'

So I reckon I got the better o' that li'l argiment.

However. The day come, and I had to go to Plymouth fer this-yer ordeal. And I can tell 'ee I was wishing all the way that zummat would hap'm to the train. Not fer anybody to be hurted, but so's us couldn' get there in time. But nothing did'n hap'm. It never do when you wants it to.

My instructions was to be to the Royal Hotel half-arter-twelve to view the ten maidens which had bin choosed out fer final. When I got inzide the hotel I stood there like a fule frightened. 'Tis a masters gurt plaace, and I was 'feared to go very fur from the door 'fraid I should lost mezel'. However, while I stood there gapping, the edditer gen'lman come and spoke to me and showed me where to hang up me hat to, and I veeled better arter that. 'Tis wonderful what a differnce hanging up anybody's hat do make. While you'm stood with yer hat in yer hand you veels a fule, cus everybody railizes that you dunnaw what to do nex'. But once you've got rids of yer hat you'm more at home, like.

'Come in yer, Mr. Stewer,' he says. 'Us have got a rume all to ourzel's, and the lunch will zoon be ready.'

111

I was mortle plaised to year he say us had a rume to ourszel's, cus I thought 'twould give me chance to pick up a vew wrinkles before us had to meet the purty maidens.

Bless yer art! Soon's I put my nose inzide the door, there they was, all the lot aw'm. Sot around waiting to be jidged they was; and me plomp right in the midst aw'm. I never was in such a position in me life. I did'n knaw which way to turn. Wherever I looked, there was a purty maiden staring me in the faace. Properly took my breath away.

And then the edditer gen'lman marched me around to shake hands with 'em, one to a time. I veeled about as comferable as if I was being walked around the wile-baist shaw and being took into the cages of the lions an' taygers. Very nice maidens they was, though, and they all smiled to me. But that id'n very much to be wondered at. If I lookid half such a fule as I veeled I must a-bin enough to make a cat laaf.

And then he introduced me to the other two jidges. One was a laady called Mrs. Wagner, o' Plymouth. A rale proper lady her was, cus her made a feller veel at 'ome in a minute. And t'other was Maister Glover. You've yerd of he fer certin. He'm a gurt man I believe. Well, anybody cude zee he is. They tell'th me that 'most everybody up to Lunnon know'th Jimmy Glover. And he was able to putt me up to a gude many tips, cus o' cou'se, he've zeed more purty maidens in one week than I shude in ten years, in a manner o' spaiking.

'Now, Jan,' the edditer said to me, 'you've got a bit o' spare time bevore lunch; go around and converse a bit to the maidens and make up yer mind which is purtiest.'

My dear zaul! If I did'n come out all over in prespiration. What could I converse about to a purty maiden, with nine more looking on and waiting their turn? You tell about Daniel in the lions' den. I'll make a bet he'd sooner be there than picking the best looking out o' ten maidens. I would, anyhow. At laiste, I thought so at the beginning, but 'twad'n so bad arter a feller got more accustomed to it.

I couldn' fer the life o' me think of a subjic' to talk about. However, zummat had to be done, so I thought if I said 'twas a vine day I couldn' go very fur wrong, and p'r'aps zummat wude turn up arter that to keep things gwain. So I picked out the one handiest the door and said 'twas a vine day, and her agreed 'long o' me, so that was the end o' that and I hadn' got nothing else to go on with. However, her'd got more sainse than what I had, by ever so much, and her started a conversation, and us got on amazing. Nice maid her was, sure nuff, and I said to mezel,' 'That's fus' prize fer certin.'

Wull then I went and told the nex' one 'twas a vine day and I soon found 'twas a lot aisier matter than what I anticipated, cus you only wanted to give 'em a start and they'd do all the talking that was necessary. 'Twad'n sich a bad job arter all.

But the beggar aw't was, I wad'n getting no forader with me jidging. Every time I went talking to a fresh maid I reckoned her was the 'ansummest. And 'genst I'd been all around the lot I was vurder behind than I was when I started.

'Darn it all,' I thought to mezel', 'I waun' have nothing to say in the matter. I'll leave it to the rest, and abide by what they thinks.'

When us sot down to dinner, or lunch I shude say, the jidges had a taable to theirsel's. 'Wull, Jan,' says the edditer, 'which is your choice?'

'Aw, no,' I says. 'Let's year the others fust. I ban't nobody to be considered.'

'The rest have all choosed,' he said. 'Us be only waiting fer you, now.'

Caw! That was a nasty one.

'Never mind about me,' I says. 'I'll abide by the mayjolity.'

But they wouldn' have that. I mus' say which I thought.

Wull, if you understand me, I did'n hardly knaw what to go by. If 'twas a hoss I'd knaw if he was yaw-neckid, or wind-broken, or a bit over to the knees, or if he had ringbone or sandcrack or aught like o' that. But when it come to a purty maiden I did'n knaw zac'ly what the points was.

'Well, Mr. Stewer,' they said, 'you mus' go by their eyes and their nawse an' mouth an' hair, and their colour and teeth, and all like o' that.'

'That daun' help a body very much,' I says. 'They've all got hair and they've all got two eyes and by the way they'm getting on with their dinner, they've all got middling gude teeth. I reckon I'd better go around again bim-by and have another look.'

Wull, arter dinner, or lunch rather, the maidens all went out in the plaace they calls the Palm Coort. A butiful plaace that was, sure nuff, like being in a king's pallis. And 'twas better light, 'cus 'twas a glassen roof up over. And the waiter-chap took us out zome caufee. I spause he overlooked it when us was inzide.

113

'Aw,' I says, 'I can zee 'em better now. I'll zoon tell 'ee which is which.'

But 'twad'n so aisy. Fust I'd think 'twas thees one, and then I'd think 'twas thikky. However. To-last I got 'em down to three, but I cude'n made up me mind which was best out o' that lot.

'Well, Jan,' says the edditer, 'have 'ee made up yer mind 'eet.'

'I have, and I ab'm,' I says.

'What do 'ee mean, you have and you ab'm?'

'I can tell 'ee which I thinks is the fus' three.'

So I pointed they out, and I'm jiggered if I wad'n same mind as the rest o' the jidges. I was some glad, I can tell 'ee.

So then 'twas only a matter which order they shude go in, and us settled that in a vew minutes. Then I zeed Maister Edditer stand up like's if he was gwain to make a spaich.

'Yer,' I says, 'what be you gwain to do?'

'I be gwain to announce the verdic',' he says.

'Aw, be 'ee' I says, 'well, hold 'ard a minute and let me get out. There's ten maidens yer,' I says, 'and you'm gwain to tell nine aw'm that I said they wad'n gude-looking as t'other one. I reckon I've been middling brave,' I says, 'to do what I have done, but I ban't brave nuff to faace that.'

So I took me hat and come away.

HOW THE WIRELESS WORKS

Jan's nephew installed a wireless receiving set, and having demonstrated its principles to his uncle the latter now finds himself in a position to explain the secrets of the wireless to other people: which he does as follows:

You may depaind there's hunderds o' volks what has got they there old wireless machines in their houses, and they dunnaw a bit how they'm worked. They harkens to the noise coming out from the machine, but they dunnaw how it gets in there.

Well, now I've had it all explained to me and I'll explain it to you.

The fust thing I've larned (which I did'n know bevore) is this-yer. They ole wirelss contraptions which so many volks has got now-a-days, is only what you might call 'half-an'-half.' They only does their work one way. Like ole Bill Maggs with his missis, you can yer what's being said but you can't putt in a word yerzel'.

They ban't like the ole telephone fer instance. Now, with the telephone, you can harken to what the t'other chap's talking about, and then you can answer 'n back. But you can't with the wireless. Aw, no! With the wireless you can yer what is said to 'ee but you can't spaik yerzel'.

Or, when I say you can't spaik, of cou'se you can spaik if you mind to, but nobody can't yer what you'm saying of. And 'tis just so well too, zometimes, when the ole machine won't work proper.

Aw, no! If you wants to go in fer what I calls the 'noise-making' part o' the business, you must have a plaace properly putt up for the purpose. And it costis a lot o' money to putt up one o' they noise-making plaaces. So there's only a few aw'm about. Well, matter o' fac', the government waun' allow very many, cus if they was to, the air wude become so full up o' this-yer ole wireless traade 'twouldn' be fit fer anybody to braithe.

Well, now, there's differnt terms fer thase-yer differnt capers. If you only goes in fer the harkening-in part, like most people do, that's called 'deception.' And the thing you do's it with is called a 'desayving set.'

But where they goes in fer the noise-making part, like the zinging and musicking and all that there, that's called 'transgression.' And the plaaces where they do's that to, is called 'Broadcasting stations.'

The principal one o' thase-yer Broadcasting stations is up to Lunnon. That's where they makes most o' the transgressions to. Then there's others about, like one to Bournemouth, and one to Cardiff and one to Plymouth. And then there's zome in furrin parts like Glasgow and Aberdeen.

Well, fust, I must' explain to 'ee how this-yer transgression business is worked.

The fus' thing you've got to have, into the Broadcasting station, is a tremenjis quantity of li'l things called 'ossylations.' They'm very important, they be, cus 'tis they what do's all the mischief.

They'm turrable small, thase-yer ossylations be. Turrable smaal they be, sure nuff. Well, this'll tell 'ee how smaal they be. If you was to have tain hunderd thousan million o' they there ossylations, and you was to stand 'em up to a heap, they wouldn' make a pin's point, all the lot of 'em. So that's why you can't zee 'em flipping about up in the air, cus they'm so smaal they ban't visible to the naked yer.

But the marvellous thing about they ossylations, although they'm so smaal, is the rate they can travel. Caw! Inzide a bit o' wire they can go like winky. Well, this'll tell 'ee how vast they can travel. If you was to have a bit o' wire a hunderd mile long (and that's a middlin' long length fer a bit o' wire) and you was to putt one o' they ossylations into one end, he'd pop out t'other end avore he'd started, 'ardly.

Ees, and 'twouldn' make a bit o' odds if 'twas tain-thousan' mile long. It daun' take a ossylation no longer to go tain-thousan' mile than what it do a lan'yard.

However he do's it I dunnaw, but he do.

Well, and now I must tell 'ee how 'tis they ossylations can travel zo vast. 'Tis because, back in the ole Broadcasting station where they comes from, the very last thing bevore they starts out on a journey, they gets a strong dose of electric *behind 'em*.

Now, you can jist imagine how that would make 'em travel. I derzay that zome time or nother you've titched one of they 'lectrisical machines yerzel'. And you do knaw how it do make 'ee hop when you gets a shock. Well now, you can quite see fer yerzel,' if you was to get that shock *behind 'ee*, all unexpected, it would make *you* travel purty quick. Well, and you must remember, you'm middling hefty, compared with one o' they ossylations. It stands to raison, if a li'l teeny, weeny thing like o' that, is gwain too get a 'lectric shock behine 'en, jist as he'm leaving home, he'm gwain a very long way in a very short time.

But the wonderful thing about they ossylations is this-yer. Although they can travel so vast through a bit o' wire, yet they can go all-so-well without it. If you had a handful o' they ossylations, and you wanted fer they to travel, us'll say from Muddlecombe to Jericho, they could do it aisy. And the way they do's it, they makes a lot o' li'l waves fer theirzel's, and then they travels on waves. Where they gets the watter to, to make the waves, I dunnaw. But from what I can understand, there's differnt sorts o' waves. There's watter waves and there's air waves, and they ossylations can travel 'pon ether.

But there's one more funny thing about they ossylations and that's this-yer.

If you was to make any soort of a noise, or a sound, like musicking, or zinging, or talking, or ort like o' that-there, so the ossylations can yer it jis as they'm leaving home to start on a journey, they'll pick up that sound, and they'll carr't along with 'em, where-ever they goes to, if 'tis ha'f ways around the world and back again.

Zo you can zee fer yerzel'. If you was to ketch one o' they-there ossylations while he'm flipping about up in the air, and you was to bring 'en up-home to yer yer-awl, you could tell what noise he was making of, and that wude be the last noise he heard back in the ole Broadcasting station where he come from.

And that's zac'ly what the volks be doing what be getting deception. Zac'ly!

And now I must tell 'ee how the deception part is done and then you'll knaw all about it.

The fust thing you got to have (that's after you've got yer desayving set, o' cou'se) is a gurt high paust sticked up in the back garden. Well, and then you haves a long length o' wire and attaches one end to the tap o' the paust and you fastens the other end to the chimley. And that's called 'air-oil.' Why they haves air-oil vor I dunnaw, unless 'tis to graise the atmosphere a bit to allow the waves to travel along a bit more suant. Well, and then you attaches another bit o' wire to the end o' the air-oil, down the zide o' the houze in droo the winder, and you fastens he on to the machine. And then you'm ready.

The objic' o' thik air-oil is to ketch they ossylations while they'm flipping about up in the air. I derzay you thinks that's a difficult job, but as a matter o' fact 'tis very aisy, and I'll tell 'ee fer why.

Although, as I told 'ee avore, they ossylations can travel on nort, as the saying is, yet they'm turrable partial to a bit o' wire. Drec'ly they sees a bit o' wire they can't resist the temtation to flip along the inzide aw'n. So, soon's ever they ketches sight o' your air-oil, they'm on it like a bird. And they flips along the inzide aw'n, down the zide o' the houze, in droo the winder, and bevore they can zay 'knive' they'm inzide your machine and they'm ketched.

But they ban't no gude to 'ee when they'm ketched, not in the state they'm in when they'm new. Fer one thing they'm so wild as a hawk. And you can quite zee fer yerzel', they there li'l ossylations, arter they've bin all they hunderds o' miles, jugging up and down on they waves, sliding along inzide they wires, pushing and shoving their way in droo your machine, they gets all out o' chune. So bevore they'm any gude to 'ee you've got to chune 'em up agean, like ole Bob Maddick with his viddle up to the dance.

To do that, you turns around a couple li'l hannles, till you've got'n proper in chune.

And then you gets the reward fer all yer hard work and all yer patience. And you can yer the lovely zinging and the muzicking, and 'tis all zo butiful, till the t'other chap comes along with his ole 'da-da-did-diddy-diddy-da-diddy-da-da,' and then you wants to go and make a vew transgressions of yer awn.

THE PARTY

With a few observations on people and manners and some remarks on dress.

'What's matter with you 's-morning, Jan Stewer?'

'What do 'ee mean, Mrs. Snell? Nothing the matter with me that I knows by.'

'Looks to me as if you could do with a pair o' spreaders to keep yer eyes open,' her says. 'Anybody wude think you had'n been to bed fer a week o' nights.'

"Tid'n hardly so bad as that, missis,' I says. 'But 'pon me zaul 'tis next akin to it. Too many laate nights to do anybody any gude. 'Twas upright vower when us went up over stairs, 's-morning, and gone dree o'clock the day bevore. I daun' mind telling you I shall be glad to go to bed raisonable time to-night, and get a bit o' buty-sleep.'

'You ab'm got nobody bad home, have 'ee?' her says.

'Us ab'm got nobody bad, missis. But if there's many more o' thase-yer ole party capers there waun' be anybody very much gude.'

'Aw, been gadding about to parties, have 'ee?'

'Zeeming to me it have been nort else but gadding about to one place and another, laately,' I said. 'Too much of it fer my liking.'

'Well, what makes 'ee do it, then?' her says. 'I spause you can plaise yerzel' whether you goes or no.'

'You can in a sort of a way, and you can't in a sort of a way,' I says. 'The young volks expec's to go where there's a bit o' merrymaking Christmas time, and 'tis only once a year as the saying is, so anybody daun' hardly like to hineder 'em from gwain to parties when they've got the chance. So I goes along, too, jis to take 'em back home when 'tis all over.'

119

'I zee,' says Tom Zalter, 'you daun' go to plaise yerzelf. Only fer the sake o' the missis and the maid, like?'

'That's zummin like it,' I says.

'Yes, but not very much,' says Tom. 'You better-way tell that tale to zomebody what don't know 'ee quite so well as what I do.'

'That's right, Tom Zalter,' says Mrs. Snell. 'Us have yerd ducks quack bevore. Jan Stewer never wouldn' go to a party if other volks did'n drag 'en there, would 'er?'

'No, he wude'n,' says Tom. 'And he never wouldn' go home again if other volks did'n drag 'n away, neether.'

'What do you mean?' I says.

'What I zay. 'Tis all very well fer you to tell up that ole logic. But you wants to tell it to zomebody differnt to me. You was to the party to Ned Annaferd's t'other night, wad'n 'ee? Yes. And what time did your missis start trying to get you to go home? When come twelve o'clock her said her reckoned 'twas time to zee about getting home-along. And her said it all over again at one o'clock with a few extry verses drowed in. And two o'clock her putt a whole chapter on to it.'

'I be quite well aware o' that,' I says. 'But then, I knaws her daun' mean it when her says it. Her daun' want to go, railly, only her likes to make out her do, so's her shall be abble to putt the blame off on to me. I only stops out o' kindness. I plaised her a lot more by stopping on than if I'd a-went.'

'I dunnaw very much about plaising her,' says Tom. 'Looked to me more like as if you was plaising yerzelf, the way you was carr'ing on.'

'What was he up to, Tom?' says Mrs. Snell.

'Up to? Well, two o'clock in the morning he was kissing Mrs. Annaferd, in under the miseltoe.'

'You lying toad, you,' I says. 'I wad'n doing no-sitch thing.'

'Yes, you was,' he says. 'Did'n you ketch Mrs. Annaferd hold bevore the eyes of everybody and arm her right in under the miseltoe?'

'No, I did'n', I says, 'and I shan't allow you to say sitch things; you ner nobody else. You wants to be a bit more careful, my vine feller, taking anybody's chara'ter away like that. You'll be getting yourzel' in trouble, else. I never went near Mrs. Annaferd two o'clock in the morning. That was Mrs. Webber to Li'lhayes. 'Twas only jis turn twelve when I kissed Mrs. Annaferd.'

'You gurt stoobid,' says Mrs. Snell. 'What odds do it make what time 'twas?'

'I likes fer anybody to tell truth while they'm about it,' I says. But I had the laaf of Tom Zalter fer once.

'Where was 'ee to last night, so laate?' says missis.

'Last night? Aw, that was to Mrs. Tucker's.'

'My jaly! I'll make a bet 'twas some party, if 'twas too Mrs. Tucker's.'

'Ees, they orwis do's the thing proper,' I says. 'None o' yer cup o' tay and a zan'witch behind the door over there. 'Tis everything slap-up, and the same as they do's it up to Lunnon. And a feller mus' be all the time thinking about behaviour.'

'How did they come to invite you, Jan? I did'n knaw you was in their category.'

'I did'n, neether. I ban't, fer the matter o' that, and shud'n wish to be. 'Tis too much wiping yer butes, and feeling if you've got yer pocket-ankcher all right, and wondering if you'm doing the right thing, and sounding the haitch in 'honner' and all the rest aw't to plaise me. But they knows that Jane and the Young Jan have picked up thase-yer jim-crack dances what they do's now-a-days, and I suppose they thinks if they invites they they must invite me. There was turrable excitement with mother and the maid about what cloas they should wear, and they went up to Exeter same purpose so's they should be properly in the fashin.'

'I yeard somebody say that Jane looked a real swell,' says Mrs. Snell.

'I spause her lookid all right fer they what be accustomed to it,' I says. 'But I tell 'ee straight when fust I ketched zight of her bevore us started 'twas touch and go that I had'n tooked off me hat an' rayfused to go along with her. I thought her'd come downstairs bevore her was raddy.

'"Look sharp and finish dressing yerzel'," I said. "Us'll be late else."

'"I be ready," her says. "I've only got my coat to putt on."

'"What do 'ee mean, ready?" I says. "You ban't gwain like that surely to gudeness. Ban' 'ee gwain to wear nothing up-about?"

'"Daun' be silly," her saith. "You daun' have no more'n this fer aiv'mins."

'"Daun' have no more!" I says. "You couldn't have very much less, fer certin. You'll be the table-talk o' the plaace."

'"Rummage," says Ann, "that's very moderate fer a party frock."

'"Party frock, do 'ee call it?" I says. "Part of a frock *I* should call it; and not the biggest part, nuther."

'But laur bless yer art, when us got to the plaace and zeed what dresses the rest o' the laadies had got on, and what they had'n got on, I'm jiggered if Jane's wude'n a-made two of some aw'm. I said to my Ann, I says, "Well," I says, "I reckon the men-volk ought to a-come in braces and shirt-sleeves and then us would a-bin about a match."

'Ole Reubin Lay made me laaf. He was stood up one end o' the rume, taking it all een, same's he gener'ly do in his ole-vashin way. "Jan," he says, "I be very glad to zee that so many o' the laadies have took notice o' what the paasen said into the pole-pit las' Zindy."

'"What was that then, maister?" I says.

'"Wad'n you to church?" he says.

'"I was," I says. "But I daun' mind nothing more'n the usual."

'"Why," says Reubin, "the paasen said us ought to try zometimes and zee what us can do without. I reckon zome o' thase-yer laadies be carr'ing that out proper. They cude'n do without very much more, fer certin."'

'I dersay they looked very nice, now.' says Mrs. Snell.

'Aw, ees, they looked nice nuff,' I says; 'they what it suited. But 'twas summat like Reubin said. Sevverl aw'm wude a-bin a lot more sainsible if they'd covered theirsel's all over. "Jis look at ole Sophy Dipcott, Jan," he saith. "Her putts me in the mind of the raymes of a turkey arter two dinners and a supper have been had off it. And there's poor ole Miss Shipway, lookee. Her's like the carving-fork tettyvated up with the frill off the 'am-bone."

'"I spause her's hoping to ketch a man," I says.

'"If her do," says Reubin, '"twill be by getting one hitched up in her shoulder-blades. And that's what's gwain to hap'm if her id'n very careful. They'm like a pair o' gurt vish-'ooks poking out."

'That's the way he was keeping on all the time; and expect anybody to keep a straight faace.'

'Had'n he got nothing to zay about the men-volk?' says Mrs. Endycott.

'Bless yer 'art, 'ees. He had'n got no more patience with zome o' the men than what he had with the women. Speshly they what was trying to mimic the bettermos' volk and carry on with a passel of fantysheeny ole crams which did'n belong to 'em.

122

' "Jis' look to Tom Weslake's boye," he says. "He've bin stidding zo much aristy-crockery that he've gone aristy-cracked. Bowing and scraaping, he is, like a merry-ander. If he grins very much more the top part of his haid will vall back over. Gude-looking veller if he'd let his faitures bide natteral: but he've had his faace tied up in knots ever zince he've bin in the rume. He'll have a job to get'n straight again if he id'n careful. And there's young Arry Laiker. In burches and liggins he looks a man, but in thik rig-out I'm jiggered if he id'n more like Varmer Urferd's mommet." '

'What rig-out was that?' says Mrs. Snell.

'Aw, most o' the men-volk had on thase-yer claw-'ammer coats with the front part cut out and hanged on behind. Arry must have borreed his off a chap about half his size, and he looked like a sossidge what had oozed out yer and there in the frying. And zome aw'm was jist the oppozyte, like a robin in a weelbarra.

' "Most aw'm is like me, Jan," says Reubin; "they'd be a zight more comferable if they was to come in the zame cloas they goes to work in. This-yer vanciful rig-out is all very well fer they what be suited to it, but I'd zooner be in me shurt-sleeves, mezel'. 'Cou'se, women-volk daun' matter how oncomferable they be so-long as they'm differnt to everybody else. But this-yer hard ole shurt like a planch on yer chest, and the bissly ole coller cutting anybody's yers like a knive only erritates me."

' "What makes 'ee dress like it, then, maister?" I says.

' "Fer paice and quietness' saake, Jan," he says. "Ever zince us made a bit o' money and got up in the higher spear as they calls it, my wive and darters insists that I shall go about trigged up like a pervorming monkey. Of cou'se, I could rayfuse and bide 'ome, but 'tis question which is the laist botheration; and I've come to conclusion, taking all things in consideration, that 'tis better fer me to zuffer a nower or two yer, than what 'tis to putt up with the nagging of a paasel of women fer a week.

' "You zee, Jan," he says. "where 'twas to, I daycided that my darters should be larned to be laadies, and now, begad, they've turned around and determined that I shall be a gen'lman. Wull, you knaw, us be zummat like the dogs. To train a dog proper you mus' begin with'n when he'm young. But I be got too old in the tooth to try to be aught else but rough and raddy, and 'tis rediclus fer 'em to expect otherwise."

' "You looks as much a gen'lman as any body in the rume, maister," I says. And I'm bothered if 'twad'n true, too.

'"Ees, Jan," he says; "I be like a lot else, I shall be all right so-long as I keeps me mouthe shut. But 'tid'n everybody have got the sainse to do that. Some aw'm ab'm got the gumtion to bide on ground where they'm safe and they goes rishing into plaaces where they daun' know their way about, so they very zoon bumps into zummat. Why should us try to look differnt to what us be? There's young Robert Zellick over there, lookee, he'm dressed up like Lord Bug in a Band Box; and he looks about as vitty as a cow in a church.

'"This is the third time I've zeed they clothes he've got on since Christmas, and it have been a differnt feller inzide 'em every time. And I'm blest if I knaws which o' the three looked the most oncomferable."

'"I dersay 'tis your mistaake, maister," I says. "How could you knaw 'twas the zame clothes?"

'"Cus there's a li'l plaace back o' the coat where he've bin broke zome time or 'nother and stitched up. You can zee 'en fer yerzel' if you looks. I owned 'n in a minute. Poor Robert is veeling about as cule and comferable as a blacksmith working in two top coats. I yeard'n jis' now axing his mother to let'n have a hankercher cus he'd come away without other-one. Her told'n her putt one in the pocket when her brished the clothes.

'"'You cude'n do that,' he says. 'cus I ab'm got no pocket.'

'"'I tell 'ee I putt one in the pocket in the tail o' yer coat.' her says.

'"'Aw,' he says, 'is there a pocket in the tail o' me coat? What a stoobid plaace to putt a pocket to.'

'"Zo he started grawping about, behind his back, and it took'n I dunnaw how long to vind his hankcher and twice as long to putt'n away again. There he is now, lookee zee, trying to get his hankcher again. See how he'm stretching back around to vind the pocket! He looks zac'ly like a dog wth a flea where he can't come at'n. If he reaches much more he'll go right back over fer certin. There, look-zee, his hand keeps coming out droo the placket-'ole. Aw, now he'm gwain to putt the other hand round to assist. That's right, Robert, stop'n with one hand while you ketches 'n with t'other. Now he've got'n to-last. I shude tie 'en around me neck if I was he, sooner than have that ole caper every time."'

'I reckon they did'n all look zo stooobid as you'm trying to make out,' says Mrs. Snell.

'You'm quite right, missis,' I says. 'To my way o' thinking zome o' the varmer's sons lookid the equal to any o' the nobs in the rume, and 'twas marvel to me the way they was able to carry it off. But they was the ones what did'n try to make theirsel's conspishus, and did'n matter what other volks was thinking about 'em. When they was containt to be natteral they looked as well as the next. 'Twas when they tried to be unnateral that they made theirsel's redeclus. Same as when Robert Zellick tried to make a bow to Miss Julia Tucker like he'd zeed a chap do in the picshers. They trousers he'd borreed was a bit on the long zide fer'n and he'd got his braces up middling tight. Zo when he bent hiszel' purt' near two-double one o' the back buttons come off. And 'twad'n to say that Robert could hide the fac'. He'd choosed a time when everybody was sot around waiting to start the dance, so's they should all zee that he knawed the way to do it proper. Went right across the vloor he did, to where Miss Tucker was sot to, and everybody watching aw'n. Made a bow he did, as if he'd got a turrable pain in his stommick. And thik button did'n come off quiet, like buttons will zometimes. It bust off with a pop which could be yeard all over the rume. And Robert made it wiss by putting up his hand to the place, quick, and shutting his top teeth down over his bottom lip. The ladies what did'n have to laaf must have suffered purty bad in their inzides.'

'Strikes me,' says Mrs. Snell. 'you and Mr. Lay had a vine ole time critikising other volks. But what about yerzel's, I shude like to knaw.'

'Aw, us looked arter oursel's all right, missis.'

'I'll make a bet you did. Trust the both of 'ee fer that. But I hope the drinks was better than your behaviour. Well, there, they must a-bin. You'd never have bide there till that time o' night else.'

125

TWENTY TO ONE

How Tom Salter received some valuable tips at Barleycombe Races.

'Did I go the raaces!' says Tom Zalter. 'Did you say did I go to the raaces? My dear zaul!'

'And winned a fortin, too, Tom, they tells me,' I said.

'Aw, yes; I winned a fortin all right,' says Tom. 'And if I'd winned many more fortins o' the zame soort I should soon be in Union.'

'Wull,' I says, 'I only knaws what I yeard. My missis told me, and her had it from your wive's awn lips, that you winned twenty to one, or zummin like that.'

Ole Tom zot chowing fer a bit, and never said a word; only stared at nothin', with one eye shut.

'What, be trying to remember zummin you've fergot?' I says.

'No, Jan; I be trying to ferget zummin I've remembered.

'I mid-so-well let you into a saycret,' he says, arter he'd stared a bit more. 'I'd ax you to promish not to tell anybody else only I knaws it wouldn' be no gude. But I spause 'twill get all around the parrish zome time or 'nother, so I'll tell 'ee the whole rigmarole. P'r'aps 'twill larn you a lesson. It have me, anyrate.

"Twas like this-yer. I ban't a betting sort o' feller as you do knaw very well. I got to work too hard fer my li'l bit to give it away to chaps that rides about in their moter-cars and smokes cigars as long as yer arm.

'However, once a year, when I goes to Barleycombe raaces I might venter so-much as a shullin, jis' fer the fun o' thing; but never no more'n that. And even then my missis gets turrable niffy with me, cus a wumman daun' usu'ly like to bet without her's sure her's gwain to ween. So you mid depaind I was properly tooked aback when her said too me, jis' as I was on the point o' starting:

'Yer!' her says, 'stap a minute. I wants you to do zummin fer me.'

'What's that then?' I says. 'I ban't gwain buying no drapery trumpery, so I tell 'ee, straight.'

126

'I wouldn' let 'ee to,' her saith. 'You ab'm got sainse nuff fer that. There's a hoss in one o' they races called 'Door Stap,' id'n there?'

'I dunnaw,' I says. 'How shude I knaw?'

'Well, there is,' her says, 'and I be gwain to bet on 'en.'

'Wull, you could a-knock' me down with a strawmot.

'You be?' I says. 'How can you do that?'

'I wants you to do it fer me,' her says 'Take this-yer vive-shullins and bet Door Stap.'

'Vive shullins!' I says. ''tis redecklus. One's a-plenty.'

'You yer what I zay,' her saith. 'You do what I tell 'ee.'

'How do you knaw there's any such hoss?' I says. 'And furthermoore, how do you knaw he'm gwain to ween?'

'Well, I *do* knaw, and that's gude nuff. There was a gen'lman come in shop 's-morning in a turrable flummox, cus zummat had gone wrong with his moter-car, and he was in a doost of a hurry to get along. But he had'n got the proper tool, zeem-zo, to putt his car to-rights, and I carr'd in the ole tool-box from the back-'ouse, and he turned everything over and found the very right thing too mend 'en with. Soo he was able to get'n gwain again in a vew minutes. And when he took back the tool he axed me what I shude charge 'n for the use of it, and I said, Rummage, I wad'n gwain to charge nothing fer a li'l thing like that; so then he said, 'Is your man gwain to the raaces?' and I said, 'I dersay he will; he'm only too glad of any excuse to lef' work.' 'Wull,' he says, 'tell'n to back Door Stap and he'll win money.'

'Did he say was to bet vive shullins?' I says.

'No,' her says, 'he said you was to bet yer shurt.'

'Wull, he id'n worth vive shullins,' I says, 'cus he ab'm got no buttons; and ab'm had, this weeks.'

'Never mind,' her says. 'You bet vive shullins, fer me. 'Tis the last race, mind; the gen'lman said so. And zee that you brings me back all the winnings. And the vive shullins bezides.'

'Wherever do the women-volk pick up their knowledge to? Jis' vancy at her thinking o' the vive shullins as well.

'And yet, zame time, I thought to mezel', 'How stoobid women will be. Vancy her taking notice of a perfec' stranger like that. If I was to tell her a certin hoss was gwain to win her wouldn' take no more notice than if the cock was to crow.

'Be-as-'twill, I goes over to Barleycombe, and I had'n bin inzide the raace-vield many minutes bevore I rinned into James Cowley.

127

Wull, o' cou'se what James don't know about hosses id'n worth knowing. And he said to me, 'You bet on Tin Can in the fust raace, Tom. 'Tis walk-over fer'n.'

'Wull, now,' I thought to mezel', 'there's some sainse in getting a tip from a chap like James. Not like harkening to a perfec' stranger.' So I bet a shullin on Tin Can. Wull, 'twas a walk-over all right, so-fur as Tin Can was consarned. He walked over the whole course. But the others all rinned, so he come in jist in time to zee the winner's number go up.

'Wull, and jis' bevore the second race I meet with Walter Bowden. And o' cou'se, Walter have bin mixed up with that soort o' thing all the days of his life, and what *he* don't know about hosses id'n worth knowing.

'You bet on Drain Pipe in this race, Tom,' he says. 'The other hosses waun' zee which way he goes.'

'Wull, now,' I says to mezel', if Walter Bowden don't know, who do? A sight better than harkening to a perfec' stranger.'

'So I putt a shullin on Drain Pipe. And 'twas true what Walter said. The other hosses did'n zee which way he did go. But if the'd turned around and looked behind they cude a-done.

'However, jis' bevore the nex' race, who should I come up agin but Zam Goodin. Wull, Zam use to ride racing hiszel', right back so long ago as when he was groom to Squire Brown; so what Zammy Goodin don't know about hosses id'n worth knowing.

'What be gwain to win this race, Sam?' I says.

'Aw, giddout!' he says. 'There id'n but one hoss in it, and that's Quart Pot.'

'Wull, I thought that was gude enough from a chap like Zammy Goodin. Differnt to harkening to a perfec' stranger. So I went and bet a shullin Quart Pot.

'And the race had'n been gwain on very long bevore Zammy's words come true. There wad'n but one hoss in it, and that was Quart Pot all right. Long arter the rest had vinished and was having a bran-mash back in stable Quart Pot was still in it. And they had to push 'n off the coorse to-last, to make rume fer the nex' raace.

'However. The nex' two raaces I do verily believe I shude a-bin all right, and the hosses I backed would have winned, only one valled down and brock his neck, and t'other one mistook the way and lost hiszel'. He lost my shullin zame time.

'Wull, and the nex' raace was the one Door Stap belonged to. So I goes off with mother's vive shullins. On the way I meet with Enry

128

Mugferd, and o' cou'se, what 'Enry don't know about hosses id'n worth knowing.

'What be gwain to bet thees time, Tom?' says 'Enry.

'I thought about betting Door Stap,' I says.

'Caw! Did'n 'Enry laaf! Laaf! I thought he was gwain to bust hiszel'.

'What,' he says, 'have zomebody left 'ee a fortin that you wants to get rids of?'

'Daun' you think Door Stap will ween?' I says.

'Ween!' he says. 'Why, I wonder the Society fer the Preservation of Cruelty to Animals daun' putt 'em all to prisin fer latting the poor toad rin at all. Have 'ee zeed 'en? Come and look at'n.'

'So he took me in to the plaace where they laids the hosses around to keep 'em warm, and showed me which was Door Stap. And he was a proper thurdlegutted toad sure nuff.

'He'll never get around the coorse,' says 'Enry, 'never mind about ween. You back 'n if you want to,' he says. 'The bookies will give 'ee twenty to one, and only too glad to get yer money.'

'But I wad'n gwain to go contr'y to 'Enry Mugferd. 'Twad'n like a perfec' stranger.

'Which do reckon be gwain to ween, 'Enry?' I says.

'Well, look at 'em,' he says. 'You've got two eyes, ab'm 'ee? There's the winner: "Ome Brewed.' Zee the way he picks up his veet. Like as if he was made of injy-rubber. There id'n another hoss there can look at'n.'

'So I thought too mezel', ''Tis no gude chucking away vive bob, and if I bets 'Ome Brewed I can keep the winnings and 'twill make up what I've a-lost, and a bit over fer a drink.'

'They wouldn' let me have but two to one, but 'twas better to win two to one than losty twenty to one. So I bet mother's vive shullins on 'Ome Brewed. 'Her'll never knaw,' I thought to mezel', 'but what I bet Door Stap.'

'And zo they started, about a dizzen aw'm. And soon's they got the word to go, 'Ome Brewed stood up on his hine ligs and lookid all around the coorse. And I suppose he did'n like the look of it, fer he turned tail, and away-do-go in the oppozyte derection. And nothing the jockey could do would make'n alter his mind.

''Enry Mugferd said the other hosses wude'n be able to look at'n, and 'twas ture fer certin, cus 'twad'n very long bevore he was out o' sight. I reckon he mus' be about half-ways to Ostrillia by thees time.

129

'Aw, wull,' I says to mezel', 'the only thing now is fer Door Stap to fall down a rabbut-'ole or zummin. And the zooner the better fer paice an' quietness' saake.'

'But tell about falling down! I'm beggered if he wad'n like a hoss possessed. If he'd had wings he cude'n a-went no differnt. Over the jumps like a burd flying; and no more notice took of 'em than if they wad'n there. The other hosses couldn' zee which way to rin on account o' the dist he was leaving behind. When he went past the winning-paust the jockey feller was picking his teeth, and the rest o' the hosses wad'n around the bend.

'So I went off too a quiet plaace where I cude think it over, and I had a bit o' pencil and paaper to figger it all out. But 'twas beyond me, cus me mind was all to a miz-maze. I knowed 'twas no gude fer me to zay Door Stap did'n ween, cus 'twould be on all the paapers nex' day. And as fer telling mother I didn' do what her said – well, there, 'twad'n to be thought about.

'However. I ketch zight o' Mr. Wi'yum Tucker and I went up and spoke to he. 'I bag pardon, zur,' I says, 'what must anybody get fer vive shullins at twenty to one?'

'I thought he'd drap daid.

'What!' he says, 'you had Door Stap! That's vive pound you've winned. Who ever gived 'ee that tip?'

'My missis, zur.'

'Wull, Zalter,' he says. 'I shude take care of my missis if I was you. Her's worth a fortin to 'ee if her can vind 'em like that.'

'I could have gived he a scat in th yer-awl fer two peens.

'And zo I had to fork out vive pound and vive shullins of me awn hard earned zavings, and hand 'em over to the missis. Her let me have back the vive shullins and said I could keep it fer me trouble. And then her played 'Amlet cus her reckoned I did'n shaw a proper thankfulness fer't. So I had to make up a bit of a spaich and say 'twas very kind. And her all the time inspecting my pound notes to make sure they was gude.

'And then you say, did I go to the raaces!'

HISTORY IN RUINS

Lias Buzzacott, self-appointed guide, personally conducts parties of visitors to the ruins of Muddlecombe Castle. His history has worn thin in places, and his patches are a doubtful match; but everybody appears to be satisfied.

I never come across the feller to Lias Buzzacott; 'pon me zaul I never did'n. Hangallus toad he is, if ever there was one.

Say any mortle thing Lias will, and daun' matter a scrap who he says it to, nuther. He'd as leef tell up zome redecklus ole yarn to paasen or squire as what he wude to you or me or any other common body. I daun' believe Lias would odds it if 'twas the king hiszel'. He'd furbish up zome ole witpot or 'nother.

And yet fer all that, you can't take agin the feller, 'cus he never says aught to do anybody harm. He wude'n say a word out o' plaace about a body behind his back; but bevore his faace he'd tell him up any ole tale, and keep his awn features so-solemn as a jidge. 'Tis hard job, zometimes, to know whether he'm telling the truth or no. But if you make a rule to believe that he id'n, you waun' go very fur wrong.

But this-yer 'guide' caper beat everything. However he got the idaya into his haid I can't think. Well, there! How *do* the idayas get into Lias's haid? I daun' know.

You zee, now-a-days us gets scores and hundreds o' visitors to Muddlecombe, one time and another. I can mind the time, and not so very long agone neether, when if a stranger went droo the village all the parrish would be out to look at'n, and discuss who he was and where he come from and where he was gwain to and what he was on upon. But now, bless yer 'art, with so many o' they ole cherrybims coming out from the gurt towns, 'tis nothing onusual to zee as much as thirty or vowerty strange volks in the strate, all to once. And very off'n they comes from plaaces right up-the-contry

131

which us never yeard of bevore. 'Tis wonderful the distance they ole cherrybims will travel.

Wull, and o' cou'se, the strangers roams about the parrish fer a nower or zo to stretch their ligs and zee what there is to zee. And I suppaus Lias have been to zome plaace where a guide walked the volks around and explained all the 'istory, and zo he thought he'd do the zame, and take 'em up around Muddlecombe Castle.

And the things he do tell they visiters is zummat outrageous. 'Tid'n true, you knaw, not half-quarter aw't. Where ever he've scraped it all up to I can't think. I said to 'en once, 'Lias,' I said, 'how ever have you got the chick to tell up sich ole logic? 'Tis lies, half of it, and you knows very well 'tis lies. I wonder the words daun' stick in yer droat and chuck 'ee, I do.'

"Tid'n lies, Jan,' he says, 'not acsh'ly. 'Tis what I've raid in the bukes. I dersay I might have got it mixed up a bit but that daun' make it lies. If I was to putt me boots on me haid instead of on me veet you cude'n say they wad'n boots, jis' cus they was in the wrong plaace. And 'tis same with my 'istry. Fac's is fac's, and alwis will be zo. If you hap'm to putt 'em in the wrong plaace that daun' stop 'em from being fac's, any more than your hat would stop being a hat if you was to hang 'n up in apple-tree. So what's the odds?

'And bezides,' he says 'they daun' take it in. They likes to yer me praich it forth, and they gives me zixpences in galore. But they only gives it to me for my chick. They daun' believe what I tells 'em, not even when 'tis true.'

'Which id'n very auf'n,' I says.

'How do you knaw?' says Lias. 'You ab'm stidded the matter like I have.'

Be that as it may, 'tis quite true what Lias says about the visitors being amused at his ole rigmarole. I've zeed 'em coming back to the cherrybims laafing like billy-o.

'What's think o' the Guide?' they'll zay too one-t'other. 'I reckon he's better than gwain to the picshers.'

And I've knawed volks come out the secon' time and take their frien's along, to yer the Guide to Muddlecombe Castle.

I dunnaw whether you've ever zeed our castle or no? 'Tis a very old ancient plaace, although 'tis all to ruination now. But you can distinct the walls and where the differnt rumes use to be to. Years agone a party o' gen'lman come out and inspected it, and one of 'em told up all the rigmarole and pedigree to the Deb'mshur

'Sociation, and 'twas all putt into a book. Us had sevverl o' they books in the parrish, one place and another, and Lias spelled out every word of it in his spare time, which natterally helped 'n a lot in his guiding.

But he reckoned the Deb'mshur 'Sociation chap did'n putt in hardly nuff fac's to make it realastic, so he sticked a vew more of his awn 'pon top. So with what he've read in the buke, and what he've yeard, and what he've made up out of his awn haid Lias have hatched up a middling find ditty.

I went around with'n one day, jis' to zee what sort of a yarn he was telling up. There was two o' they ole cherrybims stapped to Muddlecombe fer a cup o' tay and look around, and there must a-bin thirty or vowerty people got out. Lias wad'n very long bevore he putt in his spoke.

'Any laady or gen'lman,' he says, 'that likes to visit the ruins of Muddlecombe Castle and year all the 'istry thereof, a party will start yer-from in half-hour's time under the superintention of Lias Buzzacott, official guide.'

Where he larned that oration to I can't think; but I spause he've yeard it some-place where he've been to, and of course, he've got the chick of the Ole Man hiszel'.

Wull then, the volks goes and has their tay, and Lias he pokes around in amongs' 'em and tells up some of his ole witpot and makes 'em laaf, and they takes a vancy to 'en, and by the time he was ready to start there was upperds of a score laadies and gen'lmen tailing on behind, all aiger to year what he was gwain to zay. So I volleyed on last, and kep' mezel' in the background, cus I did'n want the volks to think that I was aught to do with Lias, in case of what ole rummage he might tell up. But Lias stepped it out in front as big as bull's-bafe.

You mus' understand, the ruins be up the tap of Castle Heel, and that's a matter o' tain minutes' walk. But Lias begins his ole rigmarole soon's ever he gets inzide the gate to the foot of the heel.

'Now, laadies and gen'lmen, you'm stood to the bottom of the famous Castle Heel, where in the ole ancient times they use to vight all the gurt battles which you've rade about in 'Istry books. On the burge which you've jis' come across is where the devil fought the malster, and the gurt rock which you zees in front of 'ee is where King Alfred zot and played 'The Sailor's Hornpipe' to the Dames. You mus' understan' there was so many dames about these parts in

133

they days that they was become a proper nuisance and they did'n give the king a minute's paice, on account of his being a widda-man and every one of they dames aiger to be his number two. So as I say, he tooked along his accorjion and he zot on that rock and made 'em all dance to the music. And he kep' 'em dancing from the fus' thing in the morning till the cows come 'ome, and by that time they cude'n move another stap, and they all valled along and laid about like anybody dead. And then the king called in the Special Reserve, which was all married men, and told 'em to pick up the dames and chuck 'em into the pond which use to be to the bottom of the village; and they chucked 'em in as fur as every they could; only too glad o' the chance. 'There,' said the king, 'that'll keep the dames cule.'

'So the plaace got the name of Dames Cule.

'Years afterwards a houze was putt up on the spot where the pond use too be, and 'twas called Dameskule in memorial of the great relief which King Alfred brought to the distric'; and 'twas still called Dameskule right down to the time when my vather was a li'l boye.

"'Twas on the night bevore Ole Cursmas Day when King Alfred got rids o' the Dames, and to this day anybody passing by the spot on Twelthy Eve in the middle o' the night can year they ole women yapping in under the ground; speshly if he hap'ms to be returning back from the Black Hoss. The longer he've bin sot in the Black Hoss the more Dames he can year.

'And now us'll make our way up the heel,' says Lias; 'and I shude like fer you to take notice that you'm passing through the vield where, in the olden times, they use to hold the Wars o' Roses. They was called by that name cus nobody wad'n 'lowed to take part without he'd got a rose in his button-'awl. One side weared white roses and t'other side weared urd roses. So at the end o' the day they only had to go around and count up how many o' the daid men had white and how many had urd and they cude tell d'rectly which side had winned the battle. Otherwise they'd have to wait till the newspapers come the nex' morning.

'But the boss of the Urd Rose party cude'n understand why 'twas there was orwis more urds dead than whites when they come to reckon up. And when they come to inspect a bit more careful they vound that sometimes when a White Rose chap was killed the blid wude turn his rose into a urd one, and zo he was counted in on the

wrong zide. Zo the nex' time they held a war, all they lot turned up
with primroses instead of urd roses. And this time they winned aisy
and the King o' the White Roses was forced to hide away up in the
oak tree which you can plainly view half-ways up the heel. That was
on the nineteenth of Apprul, so ever since then the nineteenth of
Apprul have been called Primrose Day. And they did'n vind the king
up in the tree till the twenty-ninth o' the volleying month, and he'd
had nothing to ait in the maintime but oak-apples. So the twenty-
ninth o' May was called Oak-apple Day from thence-forth.

'So arter that there wad'n no more Wars o' the Roses cus they
reckoned there was too much chaiting. And the people in the
villages around had to go to the picshers instead.

'However. They cude'n go on very long wai'out vighting in they
days, so they got up another war called the Battle of Hastings,
between the King o' the Mormons and Julia Sayzer. The King o' the
Mormons was caaled Henry Eighth, and he wanted to marry Julia;
but her vound out that he'd had no less than zix wives already, so
her told 'n that her wouldn' have'n if he was covered all over in
traicle and rolled in a heap o' zovrins. So they had a war and Julia
hid herzel' away in a win'mill which used to stand on the very spot
where you'm stood to now. Her could have been took prisoner
aisy, but when the Mormons vound that Alfred had done away with
all the dames they turned their back on their king and went up on
Plymouth Hoe. So King Henry had to run fer his life, and Julia went
arter 'en in a moter-car with zyves on the wheels. And that was how
they come to vind out about the reaping machine.

'And now us be come to the Castle of Muddlecombe. As you
zees, 'tis all valled abroad to ruins now, but when 'twas fus' erected,
'twas so high that they had to take down the flag-pole on the top to
let the moon go by. On account o' the gurt heighth o' the castle the
king all but lost his fus' battle, becus the chap what was putt on top
to keep watch never give warning when he zeed the enemy coming
on hossback. And when the king went up in the lift to zee what the
watchman was up to, and why he did'n give the single that the
hossmen was coming, the watchman said, 'Caw! Be they hossmen?
I thought they was rabbuts.'

'Thought they was rabbuts, did 'eee?' says the king, who was
orwis a great chap fer a joke; 'well you go and have a closer look at
'em and zee if you can tell the differnce.' And with the zame he
ketched up the feller by his heels and tip'n right out over the zide o'

135

the castle. Vive minutes it took 'n coming down; and thousan's o' years arterwards when they was digging a well on the zame spot they found the body vifty veet below the level o' the ground. And there you can still zee the hole right bevore yer eyes to this very day, which proves that what I zay is the truth.

'Muddlecombe Castle was built in the leb'mth sanctu'ry by a gen'lman called Robert Day. 'Twas origi'ly Middlecombe, so called on account of being in between the castles of Barleycombe and Wifflecombe. But then they putt up another castle to Orcombe, and that made vower, and the consequence was they used to get in a muddle as to which was the middle, so they changed it from Middlecombe to Muddlecombe. Robert Day had twelve zons, all boyes, but the king reckoned that was too many Days in one houze so he made zix of 'em knights. Then Robert had a darter and having zix Days and zix knights already, he called her Zaturday to finish out the week. Arter that he was made a barrener and called hiszel' Lord Muddlecombe. He was very gude to the poor and use to zend the king two 'ogs-'eads o' zider every quarterday.

'Muddlecombe Castle was surrounded by eight walls, one fer each day o' the week and two fer Vridys, which Robert orwis considered was his unlucky day. And outzide that lot there was a gurt deep ditch full o' watter caaled a moat, which you can still zee fer yerzel'. 'Tid'n very much of it now, cus it have been mostly fulled in, on account of King Jan's crown being blowed off in a gale o' weend and valling in the watter, and getting all over muck and wet.

'On the spot where thik stout gen'lman is stood to, is the very plaace where King Cokanit tooked off his butes and stockings and said the watter wude'n make his veet wet cus he was a king. Of cou'se, he took care that his veet wad'n titching the watter, so for certin it cude'n make his veet wet. But some chaps around the other side lifted up the fender and let in a rush o' watter, and bevore King Cokanit could dap back out o' they way the watter was up to his knees. So he was had fer once, and 'tis reported that all the rest of his life he never smiled again.

'Of cou'se, the idaya of this-yer moat full o' watter was to keep the enemies away. But on Zindys and Gude Vridy and sich times as there wad'n no vighting gwain on they use to go ketching eels.

'And then, later on, when the enemies was all killed and there wad'n nobody left to fight, they used the moat fer dipping sheep. And they use to keep the rams up on they high banks, so they was called the ramparts.

136

'Now I wants 'ee to take notice o' this gurt stone. In under this stone there use to a gurt hole, down hunderds o' staps. And that led down to a long passage-way right in under the ground from the castle to the Black Hoss. That was putt there so's in case there was enemies all around the castle the King could flip across to the Black Hoss and get a drink. But the king discovered that every Dick, Tom and 'Arry was running back and vore along this passage when they was suppaused to be to-work, and he determined to putt a stop to it.

'So one night, jist about closing time, he give orders that the passage was to be walled up, one end. But by some stoobid mistake 'twas walled up both ends. And it so 'ap'm'd that the sargent-major and the quattermaster sargent was on their way back to the castle at the time, having stopped behind to zee that all the taps was turned off in the barrels, and of cou'se, they was walled up in the passage and never zeed again. But if you'm passing this way of a night, when the church clock strikes twelve, and you lies down and putts your year close to the ground you can hear the sargent-major's voice:

'"Company – wait for it! 'Chunn! As you were! Dress back the secon' from the lef'."

'And then you can hear sitch a banging agin the wall and calling fer the orderly corporal to open the canteen –

'Or if you can't there's a-plenty what can.'

'I suppose if you'm stood upright you can't hear it so well?' says a gen'lman in the party.

'Not so well,' says Lias. 'You wants to lay down to hear it proper.'

'Ees,' he says; 'and I reckon the more you wants to lay down the better you can hear it.'

'I wude'n say you ban't right,' says Lias. And everybody bust out laafiing.

'Now, yer you can discern where the walls of a room use to be. This was the prisin, and 'tis a vunny thing, the very fus' person to be putt in the prisin was a king.

'You yeard me mention King Jan jis' now. Well, he was the culprit. Nobody knaws exac'ly what the trouble was, but 'twas a fuss about zome tetties.

'One day a turney-feller caaled Zimon Mountferd come to the castle and said he mus' zee the king. That was King Jan. I reckon the feller must a-bin one of Barleycombe, cus there's Mountferds in there to this day. Well, this-yer feller wanted fer King Jan to sign for some Magnum-bonums.

137

'You knaws what Magnum-bonums be, fer certin. They'm a sort of tettie. Longer agone it use to be all Magnum-bonums around these parts, and Buties of Abram and all they ole-vashin sort. Now-a-days 'tis mos'ly Up-to-date and Gurt Scot and Aaron Chief and sitch like; but in they days Magnum-bonums was the most tettie they went in for.

'Be-as-'twill, Maister Zimon Mountferd said that King Jan mus' sign for the Magnum-bonums. But all the big nubs in the castle was agin it, and said that the king muzzen sign for 'em. Mind you, whether he'd had 'em or no I can't say cus I daun' know; but I wude'n say that he had'n, cus he did'n have very much of a chara'ter with the tradespeople, by all accounts.

'However. I spause he was feared what the consequences might be if he was had up and his name appeared on the paapers, so he signed for the magnum-bonums, and the turney went away satisfied. But the knights and the barreners and the rest o' the big volk in the castle, they was that vexed with him that they took and shut him up in this-yer prisin. And when they shoved him in they said, 'There, that's done Jan.'

'And zo the rume was called done-jan; and 'tis still called dunjun to thees day.

'Now, if you'll plaise to walk back around behind, you'll notice a smuthe grass plot. This is where ole Crissmas Calumbus was playing skittles when the spaniels come around the corner. Of cou'se, we shouldn' take no notice of a vew spaniels now-a-days. But spaniels was very differnt things in they times. They was big as elephants and fierce as taygers. And 'twad'n to say there was a dizzen or a score of 'em. There was thousan's, and they was ready to eat up everything and everybody. Natterally the volks all thought Calumbus was gwain to stap playing skittles and rin fer his life. But not he did'n. He putt up his spy-glass to his blind eye, which he lost through having a arrow stuck in it at the Battle o' Watterloo, and he says, 'If I daun' zarve they spaniels the zame as I shall zarve thase-yer skittles may every drap o' zider in my zeller go down like rain-watter into the drain.'

'And then he turned around to the knights and the barreners and he said, 'I'll give 'ee odds on the bodkins. Us have got time to scat down the skittles and scat up the spaniels.'

'And he did too. He killed every one o' they spaniels barrin' dree-an'-twainty. And if you glimpse down this zide o' the heel you can zee where all they dree-an'-twainty spaniels was turned into stones while they was rinning away. There they've bin ever zince and there they'm likely to remain.

'Yer you can zee the ruins of another room. This was the kitchen; and 'twas in this kitchen that King Alfred was putt to watch the pot where the sheep's-head and dumplings was boiling, by one o' they dames I told 'ee about. King Alfred was very hungerd at the time cus he'd jus' come from the Women-argy-a-lot which was the ole fashin name for the Mothers' Union, now called the House o' Commons, and so he helped himself to the dumplings. And when the dame come back and wanted to knaw where the dumplings was to, he said the sheep's-head had eat 'em while he wad'n looking. But her up with her hand and give'n a thumping gude clout; not knowing, of cou'se, who her was larruping.

'And when they told her her'd bin leathering the king, her said, 'What! If I'd knowed it was the king I'd never have lifted my hand to 'en; I'd have took the copper-stick.'

'That was the cause of King Alfred fus' taking dislike to the Dames.

'This rume us be coming into now laadies an' gen'lmen, is where Mary Quane of Scotch was locked up becus her *would* insist on blowing chunes with they ole bag-pipes. Her wouldn' give nobody a minute's paice so they shut her in there and told her if her wanted to blow anything her cude blow the bellisses. For a long time none of her friends couldn' vind out where her was to, and the Scotchmen was hunting all over the plaace to vind out where the English had hid her away; but they couldn'.

'But it so hap'm'd that there was a buttcher to Muddlecombe who was a Scotchman born and bred, but he'd come down this way in business. Wull, and one day the king sent fer this-yer Scotch buttcher to come and kill a pig. So he come up to the castle to kill the said pig. But when Mary Quane of Scotch yeard the pig being killed her thought 'twas somebody playing the bag-pipes, and her started to zing the zame chune. Soon's the buttcher yeard her zinging he recognised her voice d'rec'ly, and he left the pig with the same, and went off straight back to Scotland and told the volks where the Quane was hid away to.

'So they valled in all the Scotch sawjers and away they marched fer Muddlecombe castle with their bag-pipes under their arms; and some aw'm with swords as well. When he yeard they was coming

139

the king sent up to Lunnon fer his sawjers to come on the very nex'
train and fight the Scotchmen. But the Scotchmen arrived fust, and
when the king zeed 'em marching up the heel he was properly
frightened. 'Twas then about dree o'clock in the arternoon, and he
wad'n expecting the sawjers from Lunnon till ar-pas'-vive.

'By that time,' he says, 'us'll be all dead as mutton unless us can
do zummat to stap thase Scotchies fer a bit.'

'With the zame, he glimpsed a bill about the Wile Baist Shaw
which had been to Muddlecombe a week or two previous; the bill
was still hanged up agin the wall in the drawing-rume, cus picshers
wad'n so plentiful in they days, and they was glad to get hold to
anything o' the sort.

'So the king teared off the bottom part of the bill and went out
and sticked it up over the outzide gate, jis' bevore the Scotchies
arrived.

'Presen'ly they marched up the hill with their bag-pipes in
readiness, all aiger to start fighting. But when they come to the gate,
there was the notice sticked up:

ADMISSION HALF PRICE AFTER SIX.

So they all went back and zot down to wait till zix o'clock. And o'
cou'se, ar-pas'-vive along come the sawjers from Lunnon and killed
the lot aw'm, bag-pipes and all. And the Lunnon sawjers hopped
over their bodies and kicked the bag-pipes as fur as they could zee
'em. And that's where the game 'op-scotch come from.

'But in the night there come a tremenjis hard frost and freezed all
the watter in the ditch, so Mary Quane o' Scotch was abble to slide
across the ice and get free. But her could'n vind her bag-pipes; and
her must have zummin to blow up so her went and married a
husband.

'Wull, laadies and gen'lmen,' says Lias, 'there's heaps more I
could tell 'ee if I could think of it, but the guide have gone dry, and
the gen'lman with the cherrybim is blowing up his ole vog-'orn fer
'ee to come back. So I'll wish 'ee all gude aiv'min and and I'll hold
open the gate fer 'ee to pass out one to a time.'

JIM DAVEY AND THE RABBIT

A tale of an honest rogue who claimed to fulfil a useful purpose in the world by teaching a valuable lesson.

'What have become of Jim Davey laately?' says Mrs. Snell. 'I ab'm zeed 'n this ever-so-long.'

'And daun' want to, I reckon,' says Mrs. Endycott.

'No, I dunnaw that he's very much loss; although there's worse volks about than Jim Davey, if it comes to that.'

'You'm right there, missis,' says Tom Zalter. 'There's a gude many does a sight more harm and daun' get quarter the abuse.'

'Have he left the distric', then?'

'I reckon he have, fer a bit. Got too 'ot fer'n I 'spec. He've had to go off some-place where his faitures id'n quite zo familiar.'

'I glimpsed 'n in Exeter t'other day,' says Ned Annaferd, 'and I thought he was looking up proper smart.'

'Aw, was 'er?' says Tom; 'then I reckon zomebody have larned a lesson from 'en.'

'Cude'n larn very much from Jim Davey,' says Mrs. Endycott.

'Jim orwis use to say the oppozyte,' says Tom Zalter. 'He reckons he larns people a gude deal.'

'Only thing he every larned me,' her says, 'was to hapse all the doors and fasten up the poultry when he was about.'

'Well, id'n that zomething?' says Tom. 'A very gude lesson to larn I shude think. That was alwis Jim's argiment. 'Tom,' he says, 'volks calls me a rogue; but by gude rights they ought to call me a taicher. I ought to be classified,' he says 'along with the paasen and the skulemaster. Paasen larns 'em to look arter their zauls and the skulemaster larns 'em to look arter their minds and I larns 'em to look arter their property. And I reckon that my lesson be jist as vallyble as what their's be. But only to zee the differnce. Passen and

141

skulemaster gets paid money fer their job; and what do I get?'

'Zix months, if you'm ketched,' I says.

'Thass right, Tom,' he says. 'That's the reward anybody gets fer trying to do gude to his fellercrayters.'

''Tis a wonder he had'n went to prisin long ago,' says Mrs. Endycott. 'Proper ole hipplecrit he is, if ever there was one.'

'Well, now, missis,' says Tom, 'that's another name that Jim didn't like anybody to term 'en. He reckoned he wad'n hipplecrit. You could call 'n any mortle thing else and he would take it for compliment. But if you called 'n hipplecrit he'd get properly narked.

'Hipplecrit I ban't, Tom,' he says, 'and never wad'n. You can prove it for yerzelf. When the volks zees me coming, what do 'em zay? Do 'em zay, 'Yer's Mr. Davey I zee; now what do he want? Have he come to cut up they logs out in yard?' or, 'Do he want to round up they tetties?' or, 'Is he gwain to mend the thatch on the shippen?' or, 'Will he wish to take out the baaby in the pramm'later?' No. What they says is, 'Look out, Jim Davey's about. See that they ducks is shut up proper, bim-by.'

'That's what they says when they zees me, and you can't call that ippycritical, can 'ee, Tom?' he says. 'They knows I wud'n touch nothing that I could'n raiche; and so the putts it where I can't raiche it. And that have done 'em gude, cus if *I* can't raiche it nobody can't. So their belongings is protected. I be as gude as insurance, and less expense. But they daun' thank me fer't.

'If Doctor Jinkins charges 'em vive shullins fer a pint o' pink watter with a pinch o' pipper in it they titches their hat to 'en. Or if Buttcher Parks calls vive pound nine ounces zix pound, they invites he out to a day's rabbuting. Or if the paasen comes bagging fer money to purchase pocket-hank'chers fer the black niggers, they axes he in fer a dish o' tay or a quart o' zider, according to who's about. But when 'tis Jim Davey they jis' casts their eye out around to zee that everything's all right and nothing left lying about. So I reckon I causes 'em more benevit than all the rest putt together; I dunnaw what you thinks, Tom.'

'That's how Jim used to specify the matter, and he considered he wad'n hipplecrit cus he never tried to make volks believe that he was jis' walking around fer the gude of his health.'

'Anyway, he's a proper gude-fer-nort,' says Mrs. Endycott, 'and I'm glad us be rids aw'n fer a bit. Vrightened me out o' ten years' growth, he did, a li'l while back. Poked his haid in around the back

kitchen door, he did, late one aiv'min when I wad'n expecting to zee a
zaul, and axed if he might sleep up in tallet. Made me jump right out o'
me skin, purt' near. The chicky toad; I told 'n if I ketched 'n up in tallet
I'd putt the dogs on the tail aw'n.'

'Yes, I know,' says Tom. 'And you likewise told 'n to take care and
not go smoking up there, else he'd set vire to the hay and burn the
plaace down.'

'How do you know what I said?' says missis.

'Aw, bless yer 'art, I knows. Jim orwis use to say, 'Mrs. Endycott
have got a doost of a bark but there id'n very much bite about her.' He
sleeped up there, anyhow, and you knowed it.'

'Yes, and darn the feller,' her says; 'I'm popped, when he went out
from the kitchen if he did'n pinch a bit o' boiled vat pork off the taable
right under my very nose and carry it off, and I never zeed the gwain
aw't. And I'll sware I was looking straight at 'n every minute of the
time.'

'That's zac'ly like 'en,' says Mrs. Snell. 'If you had'n been there he
would'n a-done it. 'Twas only cus you was watching aw'n. He knowed
you'd give it to 'en if he was to ax 'ee for it, but 'tis jist his han'writing to
stail zummat right bevore yer eyes.'

'That's right, missis,' says Tom. 'Jim wude'n give 'ee thankee fer any
roguery that was aisy. But if he thought you suspicioned him and was
watching what he was up to, then he'd do his huttermost to best 'ee.
Like the time he was tooked up bevore Squire Oldaway fer pauching.'

'What was that, then?'

'Aw, Jim went out one morning for a provider.'

'Whatever's that?'

'Provider? Aw, that was a li'l bit of a stroll around; what some volks
calls a constitutional; only Jim called it a provider cus he reckoned to
walk one way to provide a appetite fer his meal and then walk back
t'other way to provide a meal fer his appetite. Well, so he went in over
Squire Oldaway's vields, there to Mill Down, where there's usually a
keeper or two about, and while he was walking along a rabbut hap'm
to cross his path. Jim never carr'd a gun in his life and he wouldn' be
bothered with a dog, but if a rabbut got in his way 'twas a seldom thing
it got out again. So 'twad'n very long bevore Jim was gwain along with
his appetite and his meal both. Appetite in his stommick and meal in
his pocket.

'And then he rinned scat into a keeper. That wad'n a rare thing cus
Jim never went a yard out of his way to avoid anybody. But this time

the keeper veeled in Jim's pocket, and found the rabbut.

'Ullaw,' he says, 'where did you get that one?'

'Had'n off a Crissmas tree,' says Jim.

'Wull, you come along o' me,' says the keeper, 'and you'll get a 'Appy New Year into the bargin.'

'So he marches Maister Jim up to the Manor and reported the caase. Squire ordered Jim to be took in 'ouze, rabbut an' all. Had'n right into one o' the swell rumes, he did, where her ladyship was to, and sevverl more ladies and gen'lmen bezides. You'd a-thought Jim wude a-bin flabbergasted to be took amongs' all that granjure, but he wad'n. He was zummat like the gipsy's jackass, never putt out o' the way. Squire Oldaway was orwis ready fer a bit o' fun, and he knowed Jim Davey of old.

'However; the keeper lied the rabbut on the taable and told up his tale. And you mid depaind it did'n lost nothing in the telling. He putt in all the li'l twiddly bits to show how wonderful he'd done his juty, and then the squire turned around to Jim and axed 'n what he'd got to say fer hiszelf.

'Wull, yer honour,' says Jim, ''tis like this-yer. It all comes of me having sitch tender veelings. I be a turrable muty-arted sort o' chap where dumb crayters is consarned. I was orwis brought up to be kind to animals, and to do fer they the same as I should wish for they to do fer me. And when I zeed thik poor li'l rabbut I veeled properly sorry fer'n, cus I could zee he'd lost hiszelf and couldn' vind his way home; and dog-tired he was, too, and lookid up in my faace that pleading, I was boun' to pick the poor li'l feller up and carry 'en; cus when I come up to 'en he couldn' walk another inch.'

'Squire had a hawful job to keep from laafing, cus he'm a very gude sport.

'But the rabbut's dead,' he says. 'How do 'ee account fer that?'

'I zee he is, poor li'l chap,' says Jim. 'But he was looking turrable bad when I took 'n up, and I spause there wad'n sufficient air for him in my pocket and he in sitch a weak state, and so he must a-got stiffled.'

'But, you rascal,' says Squire, 'the neck of 'n be broke.'

'Aw, is that so, zur?' says Jim, looking as if he was 'most ready to cry. 'Poor li'l toad; he'll never get better o' that fer certin. I must a-putt 'n in me pocket up-an'-down, and he've broke his neck trying to turn around.

'So then the squire bust out laafing and so did all the ladies and gen'lmen.

144

'Well, now, look yer, Davey,' he says, 'you clear off my property and be quick about it; and if you'm ketched in my vields again you'll be putt to prisin. I'll putt 'ee there mezelf, daun' ferget. So now you make yerzelf scarce, soon's you like, bevore I do what I ought to and zend fer the policeman.'

'So Jim he wished 'em all 'Gude morning,' and tooked up his hat and away-do-go.

'Soon's he was outzide the room they all bust out laffing again, sep's the keeper who was so-wild as a hawk.

'I had to let'n go fer his chick,' says the squire; and they all agreed wai'n. They was all amused at Jim.

'Take out the rabbut and let Peters have it fer the dogs,' says Squire to the keeper.

'But the keeper was blinking his eyes to keep 'em from jumping out of his haid, and his mouthe was like one end of a tunnel.

'Rabbut's gone,' he says. More than that he had'n got breath nuff to zay.

'My great gran-vather,' says the squire, 'if he ab'm took the rabbut right bevore the lot of us. Well, of all –.' And then he got stuck too.

'Keeper, he up with his gun.

'I'll shoot'n, I will,' he says. 'I'll shoot'n avore he gets another hunderd yards.'

'You come back,' says the squire. 'You won't do nothing o' the sort. Not for that you won't. You can wait till you'm sharp enough to ketch 'n in the ac'. Davey won this game, and I think I knows how to take a beating. I'll tell 'ee what you'll do, now. You send the boye over to Jim Davey's cottage with my compliments and a couple pounds o' pork to go along with the rabbut.'

'Rare gude sport Squire Oldaway is. He cude stand a joke so-well as the best.'

THE SELLER SOLD

Jim Davey, Poacher and rogue generally, in the temporary role of assistant to an auctioneer of doubtful character proves the efficacy of setting one thief to catch another.

They zay if you speak of the dowel you'll zee his horns. Only that morning us had been talking about Jim Davey, and I'm jiggered, when us was all in the carrier's cart ready to start back home who should come strutting along but menabs hiszel'.

But, 'pon me zaul, us could hardly own 'en, fer he was togged right up to the nines. With the vaace aw'n waished and a clane coller I'm darnd if you wouldn' a-took 'en fer the squire o' the parrish.

Jim never wad'n what you'd caal a bad-looking chap; but he was orwis so slammicking that his gude looks was throwed away, in a manner of spaiking, cus he was sitch a slouch, lookin'. But this time he might a-bin Lord Bug.

'My hyvers,' says Tom Zalter, 'if 'tid'n ole Jim Davey.'

'Mr. Davey to you,' says Jim.

'I should think so too, in they togs,' says Tom. 'Who's looking fer 'em, Jim?'

'What do 'ee mean?' says Jim.

'Nothing,' says Tom. 'Only I 'ope whoever they belongs to have got another spare suit to putt on, else I'm beggared if he waun' be 'bliged to bide a-bed.'

'I'd like fer you to know, Tom Zalter, that I come by these cloas honest,' says Jim, standing with his veet crossed and spreading out one hand on his chest and the other behind his back; like the hero chaps do on the stage when they'm looking the whole world in the faace.

'Purty late in the day to start that, id'n it, Jim?' says Tom.

'And what's more,' he says, 'I've got a-plainty o' the right stuff yer to get another sitch lot if I mind to.'

146

And with the zame, he tooked out a whole han'ful o' money from his pocket and showed it around. Properly tooked everybody's breath away. But Mrs. Snell looked turrable upzot.

'Jim!' her says. 'Whatever have you bin up to now? I'm vexed to zee it, I be railly. I've orwis said that whatever else you'd do you wouldn' take money. I'd sooner have gived 'ee zome if you was in want. Can't you putt that back where it belongs to?'

'That's zac'ly what I be gwain to do,' he says; and he putt it in his pocket. 'There,' he says, 'that's where it belongs to, so you don't need to worry, Mrs. Snell. You'm a gude soort, and if there was more like you there wouldn' be so many like me. Let's get on the 'omeward journey and I'll tell 'ee all about it.'

So, gwain 'ome-along Jim told up this-yer li'l ditty.

'Arter I'd made that li'l mistake about they pheasants which I mistook fer zome pigeons I lost when I use to go to skule, I thought I'd better-way go for a hollerdy on me own accord, instead of being beholdin' to other people for it. So I went down to Plymouth fer a bit, to zee was anything being gived away bezides gude advice.

'Wull, and one day I was straiking along through the strate, wondering what it feeled like to have a gude meal under yer weskit, when a chap come up and spoke to me. Very rispectable-dressed chap he was, with a faace that I'd trust about as far as I cude sling a cow by the tail.

'Wude you like to earn a honest shullin?' he says.

'What do you knaw about honest shullins?' I says. 'I daun' suppose you ever zeed one in yer life.'

'He laafed, which showed that I had'n misjidge' 'en very much.

'You come and do a li'l job fer me,' he says, 'and I'll give 'ee vive shullins and a gude feed. You looks as if you cude do with the both aw't.'

'I'll have the feed fust if 'tis all the zame to you,' I says, fer I was leery as a drum. So he tooked me into a aiting-houze and give me a darn gude feed, so-much as I cude tackle, and a pint o' beer into the bargin.

'Now I've finished me packing,' I says, 'you can go on with the nex' chapter.'

'So then he explained his li'l caper, and 'twas about so-honest and above-board as I anticipated it would be.

'He was one o' they octioneer strappers, zeem-zo, what goes about to differnt plaaces with a paasel of ole truck coloured up to

147

look like real; one o' they yer-today-and-gone-tomorra chaps what rents a empty shop fer a day or two and fulls 'n up with all manner of tinkeraments and tries too attrac' the gawks and make 'em buy things they don't want fer dree times what they'm worth.

'Mind, I daun' zay they'm all like that. I derzay zome aw'm be honest nuff, but this feller wude zooner come by a groat by chaiting than a guinea by hard work.

'Now,' he says, 'I'll tell 'ee what I wants for you to do, and 'tis as aisy as helping George. Zometimes when I starts selling the jewlery I can't get the volks to bid up fast nuff. They gets bashful and wants zummat to give 'em a bit of incouragement. If they zees zome other body get a rale bargain cheap they'll be more aiger to spaik up. Now, in and out, I shall putt up real vallyble articles, which I keeps for the purpose, worth a scute o' money; and that's when I wants for you to bid. I'll putt my vinger alongzide my nawse at the proper time, and when I do's that 'tis meaning fer you to bid nex'. Then if nobody daun' carry on long nuff I shall knock it down to you, and you come vore and take it and hold on to it till the sale's finished. You'll pretend you'm gwain to pay for it, but I shall write it down in a buke and ax you to bide on a bit longer cus there's gwain to be more bargains. You show up what you've purchased to anybody that wants to look, and that'll make 'em wish they'd bin a bit faster. Then I'll putt up zome ole imitation and they'll pay gude money fer't. Do you follow me?'

'I've got 'ee, I says.

'And let me tell 'ee,' he says, 'you need'n think about flipping out with none of it, cus one o' my chaps will be stood to the door watching of 'ee and he'm a sight bigger than what you be. And when 'tis all finished I shall give 'ee vive shullins. Have 'ee got the idaya all right?'

'Right fus' time,' I says.

'Thass all right, then. Now you'll have to come along to my lodgings and I'll trig 'ee out in a vine suit o' togs, cus it wouldn' do fer a rough-looking toad like you to go bidding fer goold watches.'

'So he tettivated me up in thase-yer go-to-meetings, and then he tole me to trapes about a bit and look into the sale all casual like.

'Soon's ever I got out in strate, off I goes like a long-dog to ole Nathan Ball. That's my cousin you've yeard me tell about, what keeps the pawn-shop. I had'n zeed Nathan fer years, cus he've gone up in the world and mixes with a lot o' the better-most volk in the way o' business. He was middling surprised to zee me, you mid depaind. Speshly me looking as if I'd escaped from the Houze o' Laurds.

'Nath,' I says, 'you knowed me very well longer agone; did ever you know me do any gude to mezelf?'

'No, Jim,' he says, I dunnaw that ever I did, very much,'

'And did ever you know me do any harm to me friends?'

'I never knawed 'ee serve a friend a durty trick, if that's what you mean.'

'No, and you never won't. Wull,' I says, 'I wants fer you to give me the lent of ten pounds till bim-by o' night, and I shall let 'ee have it back again and another one on top o' that for interest.'

'O' cou'se, he thought I'd gone maazed, and I had a turk of a job too make'n believe otherwise. However, I persuaded him for ever so long, and to-last he let me have the money.

'Then I goes off to Dick Trimlett. You remember Dick Trimlett. He went from Week parrish and joined the police. I orwis likes to keep in with the police, in case I might meet with a bigger rogue than mezelf which id'n likely; so I knowed where to vind Dick to.

'Be you on juty this arternoon, Dick?'

'No, Jim, I ban't. Why vor?'

'Never mine 'why vor.' You put on yer private cloas and come along o' me. You'll zee a bit o' fun.'

'So he did that, and us went along to the sale.

'Us waun' go in both together, Dick,' I says. 'You go in fust and I shall walk in casual, like a perfec' stranger; only you watch everything that goes on.'

'So Dick goes in and stands in the crowd, and arter a bit I jis lookid in to zee what was gwain on.

'Mister man was stood up on a bit of a platvorm with his coat off. And I should think he must a-bin having a poorish time, cus he was baaling hiszel' black in the faace. Soon's ever he zeed me come in he putt up his vinger, meaning fer me to bid. And with the zame he reached down and took up a watch from in under the counter.

'Now, you people,' he says, 'who've been putting yer hands in yer pockets and keeping 'em there, I'm jis gwain to zee what you be made of. I can't zell 'ee nort so I'll zee if I can give it away. If you can't speak let's zee if you can hold up yer hands and take zomething fer nothing. 'Pon me word, I dunnaw how zome of 'ee manage to eat yer dinner: you mus' do it without opening yer

mouthes, that's a sure thing, cus they've bin shut so long the hinges
has got risty. Now I'll tell 'ee what I'm gwain to do with 'ee. I'm gwain
to putt up this rale gold watch, 'all-marked with a lion as big as a
dunkey, plain nuff fer the biggest dunkey to zee, a rale gold watch fit
fer the Laurd Mayor o' Lunnon to wear to his awn funeral. Look at it;
a gold watch, and he's gwain to the highest bidder never mind if 'tis
the price of a bunch o' carrots. Now then, I suppose you can open
yer eyes if you can't open yer mouthes, so stop scratching yerzel's
and take a look at'n. How much for the rale gold watch. Anyboody
say ten shullins fer the solid gold watch?'

'Zeb'm an' zix,' I says.

'GONE!' And he fetched down his 'ammer with sitch a whack he
purt' near made 'em jump out o' their boots.

'Aw, woke 'ee up have I? I'm sorry if I disturbed 'ee. You zee
what's hap'm'd while you've bin asleep, daun' 'ee? A solid gold
watch gone fer zeb'm and zix; and if the purchaser will bring 'n up to
me arter the sale I'll give'n vive pound fer his bargin. That'll be vower
pound twelve an' zix fer staying awake. Zome of 'ee wants to rub the
sleepers out o' yer eyes. What name, zur?'

'Davey,' I says.

'Mr. Davey,' he says, and wraut it down in a book. 'Pass over the
watch to the gen'lman, Bill, and let'n zee what he've got fer dree
half-crowns. Daun' pay fer't now, zur; pay me arterwards. I wants for
you to stop and I'll zell 'ee zome more bargins bevore I've done. The
man what keeps awake this-arternoon is gwain to be glad he's alive.
I'll make anybody rich that likes to risk a bit o' money. You need'n be
ashamed to let anybody zee thik watch, zur,' he says. 'You can wear it
when you goes to Buckingham Pallis and not be afraid to take it out.'

'Wull, 'twas a butiful watch, sure nuff, and there was plenty ready
to bite off their tongues that they had'n bid. But o' cou'se, they
wouldn' have had it if they had; but they did'n knaw that.

'So then the feller putt up a lot of ole trade that was like a wart on
the nawse, neether ornament ner use. And volks was bidding dree
times what 'twas worth, zame's he said they would. Then arter a bit
they beginned to quiet down again, so he rubbed his nose and putt
up a diment ring. He knocked thikky down to me fer thirty shullins
and putt'n down in the book along o' the watch. 'Twas a lovely ring,
and properly made the people's mouthes watter. By that time 'twas
mostly a fresh lot o' people, and when they got a bit slow he carr'd on
the zame caper again.

'And bim-by I'd a-got a zilvern taypot, a butiful clock in a leathern caase, a dizzen zilvern spunes, a laady's gold bracelet and a thing to go around her neck and a brooch with diments of every colour you cude mention, and sevverl more things bezides. Altogether I'd bid up nine pound odd.

'So I thought I'd got about nuff, and I was getting tired, so I goes up to the feller and says:

'Beg pardon, maister,' I says, 'I can't bide yer no longer and I've purchased all I requires so if you'll plaize to tell me how much I owes 'ee I'll let 'ee have the money and go with the zame.'

'Aw, that's orright, zur,' he says, not ketching my meaning zac'ly; 'you jis' leave the things there on the taable and let me have your derections and I'll zend my man with 'em and you can pay he when he brings the articles.'

'I won't trouble you to do that,' I says, 'thank'ee all the zame. I'll take 'em along with me if you'll plaise to make me out a bit of a bill.'

'And with the zame I takes out the ten pound from me pocket and hands it to the chap. ''tis nine pound odd, I make it,' I says.

'If I was to tell you that thik feller went all the colours o' the rainbow I wouldn' be telling one word of a lie.

'I can't attend to you fer a minute,' he says, 'Jis' wait in behind the desk till I finish the sale. I'm finishing now drec'ly.'

'I zeed'n give a look across to the big feller to the door, and he started moving over towards me.

'I'm vexed I can't stap no longer,' I says, 'cus my friend yer is a policeman and he've got to get away and report to his superintendent.'

Dick looked up to the feller an' smiled. Anybody could zee he was a bobby by the cut of him.

'Aw, my dear days! 'Tis useless fer me to try to discribe what thik cheap-jack feller was like. He cude'n deny but what the things was all knocked down to me fair and square, and he never bargined that I shude have the money ready to pay for 'em. He tried to say zummat suiting the occasion. But only his mouthe went up and down; no noises did'n come out.

'Jis' then, one o' Dick's mates passed by the door all togged up in his univorm, so Dick give'n the tip to step inzide. That finished the contrac'. I said to the feller:

'Never mind about the change, mister. You can keep that. 'Tid'n very much I know.'

'And with the zame I walked out o' the plaace. I wished the chap 'Gude arternune,' but he did'n return the compliment. I daun' believe he yeard me. He looked like as if his mind was wanderin' off on zummin else; what they calls in the novel books, 'lost in thought.'

'I carr'd all my purchases straight to Nath Ball; and I took Dick along too, to assure the ole feller that I bought 'em all fair and square. He took 'em off me at market price and I let'n have back 'leb'm pound, as I said I would. And that lef' me with a nice li'l bit over and above fer mezel'.

'I went past the octioneer's plaace again nex' morning to zee if there was any more bargins gwain cheap.

'The shutters was up.'